THE SCARLET SCOURGE

The Scarlet Scourge

A Detective Story

By JOHNSTON McCULLEY

WILDSIDE PRESS

www.wildsidepress.com

The Scarlet Scourge

CONTENTS

CONTENTS

THE SCARLET SCOURGE

CHAPTER I

FRIENDS FALL OUT

MADAME VIOLETTE stood before the open window, sensing the heat which came in waves from pavements and buildings, sniffing at the stagnant air, watching the seething, sweltering humanity on the street below her.

She glanced up at the blazing sky and into a yellowish haze that seemed to be making an ineffectual attempt to counteract the work of the merciless sun.

"There will be a storm," she whispered to herself. "I can feel it—there is going to be a storm!"

Madame Violette sighed and turned away from the window, and for a moment regarded her reflection in the full-length mirror in one corner of the room. She saw a rather stout person of fifty, with an abundance of hair which was "touched up" continually, a face that knew frequent massage, hands that were well kept and often manicured. Madame Violette represented the ever-present tragedy of a woman refusing to grow old, clinging to a youth that was past and gone, seeking yet some things that had been denied her.

Her customers often had remarked how Madame Violette could arch her too-perfect brows, how she could speak in just the proper pitch, as though born to the drawing-room, and how her face always was radiant. But those things were parts of her business; they went to make up her stock in trade.

Madame Violette operated a beauty parlor on the second floor of a huge building constructed many years before and recently repaired and remodeled, a parlor that catered to both men and women, and she was wise enough to know that members of neither sex would patronize a place whose proprietor appeared aged, unkempt, and dowdy. By her daily rejuvenated beauty—she had been a real beauty once —and her never-failing optimism, she caused other women to hope that they, too, could ward off age and retain their attractiveness.

But now that she was alone in the little parlor of her living suite adjoining her place of business, Madame Violette was her real self for a time. Her face was almost haggard as she looked into the mirror. The usual smile was not haunting the corners of her mouth. The flashing light was gone from her eyes. She did not look at all optimistic; her head drooped.

"A storm—there will be a storm!" she muttered to herself again, and she spoke in a low, almost sepulchral tone and shivered at the sound of her own subdued voice.

She shrugged her shoulders as though to cast off the spell of a premonition, and then stepped quickly across the room to a door that opened into her business establishment. She hesitated there for a moment, until she was able to force the smile back to her lips and the flash into her eyes, and then she opened the door.

There was nobody in the front room of the beauty parlor except beneath a shaded light at a table in a corner, where one of her manicurists was trimming a man's nails and indulging in a mild flirtation at the same time. That meant that all the private rooms were filled, and that her other girls were busy with regular patrons. Madame Violette nodded and smiled at the man in the corner, who was a steady customer, and beamed upon the girl.

"Flirting hurts nobody, and it is good for the business," she mused.

She walked on down a little hallway and peered through the curtains into the booths where women were having face and hair treatments. Business was excellent without doubt, yet Madame Violette sighed as she retraced her steps and again sought the seclusion of her little parlor.

Walking slowly, as though fatigued, she went across to the window and drew the shade part way down until the room was plunged into semidarkness and elusive shadows played about it. Then she drew up a chair and sat down. For an instant she was motionless, and then she passed her hands across her face, sighed once more and leaned back in the big chair. She shuddered and closed her eyes.

The door from the beauty parlor was opened suddenly, and another woman came into the room.

"Oo, la, la!" she cried.

Madame Violette looked up quickly. "You—you startled me, my friend," she said.

The newcomer closed the door and strode forward, to stand with her arms akimbo, a knowing smile on her face, her head cocked to one side like that of a parrot. She was a modiste with a prosperous establishment on the ground floor, and she was known as Madame Moonshine. She was French, with a name that was hard to pronounce; Moonshine was a literal translation.

"Your face!" Madame Moonshine exclaimed, her own face assuming a tragic expression. "Is it that you have lost your last friend and have found a host of new enemies? One would think that the wolf had entered through the door and was even now sniffing at your heels! Is it that the business is bad?"

"Oh, I guess that business is as good as usual," Madame Violette replied quickly, endeavoring to smile.

"You guess? You do not know?"

"Oh, I know, of course. I have as many customers as ever, and get many good new ones every day. But Raoul really attends to the business."

"How can he?"

"I mean that he handles the receipts and pays the bills, gives me what I ask for myself, and puts the remainder in the bank."

"It is a ticklish thing," Madame Moonshine observed, "to let so young a man endure such big responsibilities, even though he is one's own son. Is it not so?"

Madame Violette's face suddenly beamed.

"But my Raoul is a born business man," she said.

"Oo, la! I have heard you say that many times before now, my friend!"

"He will be a rich man some day. I am glad to allow him to attend to all the details of the business and manage the place. Friends have told me—gentlemen who know—that my Raoul is a born financier. Only last month he bought one thousand shares of oil stock at ten cents a share and sold them again for twelve and a half cents."

"A new Wall Street lion!" observed Madame Moonshine, not without some sarcasm, which passed unnoticed. "But tell me, what made you so sad just now?"

"A storm—there is a storm coming," answered the other.

"Of a certainty!" Madame Moonshine answered. "Did you ever see such a summer day in New York, with such heat, when there was not a storm came afterward? We shall have thunder, and perhaps lightning, and—if Heaven is kind—we shall have some rain. It cannot come too soon to suit me."

"But also," Madame Violette explained, "there is some grave trouble coming. I cannot explain to you just how I feel. But I have a feeling of dread, a premonition of——"

"You have a case of indigestion!" Madame Moonshine declared, seating herself. "If Lorenzo Brayton could hear of your premonitions, he would laugh until his shoulders shook."

Madame Violette smiled. "Of course! Mr. Brayton is a practical man," she observed.

"He is all of that! A busy man! He is growing very rich—and is making others rich, too."

"How is that?" Madame Violette asked suddenly.

"What a tone you use! Is it anything so very wonderful? He is a broker, as you know, and if he gives a friend a tip as to the market now and then——"

"I see! He has been giving you tips?"

"Now and then a little one," said Madame Moonshine. "I never met him until about two months ago, when he came into my shop, with a friend who bought a blouse for his little daughter. But he has dropped in to see me several times since."

"Indeed?"

"Does it not make the heart of a woman flutter? We are widows, my friend, and yet the fire still burns in our hearts—eh? And he would be a good catch, isn't it so?"

"I—I suppose so. But, my friend, perhaps he is only being courteous and polite."

"Oo, la, la! Trust a woman, and especially a widow, to know when a man is interested more than the ordinary."

Madame Violette got up suddenly and crossed the room to the window, but she did not throw up the shade. She did not want Madame Moonshine to observe the expression in her face. She glanced down at the street, at the jostling humanity there, at the lathered horses, and at the steaming pavements, and tried to conquer a sudden emotion. When she faced about again, her countenance was inscrutable.

"The heat is terrible!" she said, as though trying to change the subject. "Surely it will storm!"

But Madame Moonshine did not intend to allow the subject to be changed.

"Did Lorenzo Brayton ever bring his friend, Peter Satchley, to your place?" she asked.

"Mr. Satchley comes here regularly for his manicure," Madame Violette said.

"There is another good catch, my friend—a wealthy bachelor. Why not look at him now and then? He's not bad for the eyes to rest upon."

"Must we talk eternally of men?"

"And why not?" demanded Madame Moonshine. "Oo, la! Listen to the timid one! You want a husband—you cannot deny it to me. We both want husbands. And since we are not silly young girls, it is best that we consider the men in the market carefully before making our choice."

"I do not feel at all like discussing the subject to-day," Madame Violette said.

"Because there is to be a storm? You and your premonitions!"

"Well, since you insist: Is Mr. Brayton very attentive, or are you merely expressing your hopes?"

Madame Moonshine giggled and pretended to blush.

"I confess that it is not time yet to wish me joy," she replied. "But a woman can read a man's mind —eh? The question now is on the tip of his tongue. But an old bachelor is very cautious—and more timid than a youth. He will gather enough courage some day."

"You seem to be sure of it," Madame Violette said.

"He has already told me that he admires the French type, and especially a woman old enough to have some common sense. And I am of the French type, am I not? You are French in your name, of course——"

"It is good for the business."

"Exactly, my friend. And your real name——"

"Matilda Gray."

"But few know that, eh? And violet is much more attractive as a color—there is romance in it. Oo, la! This Lorenzo Brayton will be quite a man when I have had him in hand for some time. Just now he is a bit timid, of course. It is easily to be seen that he has not made love to many."

"Madame Moonshine, do you mean to sit there and tell me that he has tried to make love to you?"

"It is rather a personal affair—but of course you are my friend," Madame Moonshine replied. "A sly kiss now and then, accompanying some tip as to investments and——"

Madame Violette sprang from her chair.

"Are you telling me the truth," she demanded half angrily, "or are you merely trying to torture me?"

"Torture you, my friend? What on earth is the meaning of your queer speech?"

"Have you been spying upon me?"

"Merciful heavens! Is it that you are insane?"

"It is I who have received the sly kiss now and then—along with little tips as to investments," Madame Violette declared, genuinely angry now. "And

how could you know that, if you have not been guilty
of spying?"

Now Madame Moonshine sprang from her chair
also.

"You are telling me lies!" she declared. "You are
jealous, and would make me the same. You have
set your cap for Lorenzo Brayton, have you not, and
have failed? And so you envy me who——"

"It is you who are lying to me!" Madame Violette
cried. "It is you who have tried and failed! And
you have spied on me, and are now trying to make
me think that my Lorenzo is untrue——"

"Untrue? Oo, la, la! Untrue to whom, elephant?
I tell you that he has been courting me."

"And I tell you that he is just as good as engaged
to me!" Madame Violette exclaimed, bending forward angrily, her face almost purple with wrath.
"He has given me to understand as much. He is but
waiting to conclude a big business deal before he
really speaks."

"This is monstrous!" Madame Moonshine interrupted. "That you, my old friend, should attempt
such a game! Little good it will do you in the end!
You and your fake French name!"

Madame Moonshine snorted angrily and moved
swiftly toward the door.

"You are angry because your little scheme has
failed," Madame Violette cried.

"It is you who are angry because you have lost.
Oo, la! Friend—you? Viper!"

Madame Moonshine stopped, with her hand on the

knob, and turned to face the beauty-parlor proprietor. There was a tragic look in Madame Violette's face.

"Perhaps—perhaps he is but fooling both of us," Madame Violette said. "Perhaps he is untrue to both."

"My Lorenzo untrue?"

"I have spoken the truth."

"And you think that I shall believe it? Was I born but yesterday?" the modiste wanted to know. "You and your plots!"

Madame Violette took a couple of steps toward her.

"Wait," she begged. "I believe that you have told me the truth—and I swear that I have told you nothing else. If we are being made fools——"

"Such an idea is ridiculous! As though he would look at you when he could look at me! And Lorenzo is the soul of honor," Madame Moonshine said.

"Is any man the soul of honor where a woman is concerned? Or where gold is concerned?"

"Now I cannot fathom your meaning."

"Perhaps I have been a foolish woman. But he led me to believe that his interest in me was out of the ordinary. He—he showed me how to invest. I have put my money in that rubber company of his— what money Raoul did not know about. I was not sure that Raoul would approve."

"Oo, la! Spy! That is just what I have done— put money into his rubber company. He allowed me to do so, as a great favor, though big financiers

wanted all the stock.   He even made a jest about it
—about keeping all the profits in the family——"

"Liar!" Madame Violette suddenly interrupted.
"He made that jest to me, and only last week.   Now
I know that you overheard!   We were sitting in this
very room.   I suppose you were in the beauty parlor,
snooping around the door."

"This to me?   I snoop around a door?" Madame
Moonshine cried.   "You are a detestable person,
Madame Violette!   I have wasted many good hours
in being acquainted with you!"

She jerked the door open, darted through it,
slammed it, and was gone.

"Hussy!" Madame Violette exclaimed, shaking her
fist toward the door.

CHAPTER II

THEN came the reaction, and Madame Violette threw herself full length upon a couch and gave way to a tempest of tears. But she was a woman of resource who had been compelled for some years to fight against the world for a living, and so the fit of weeping passed soon, and she bathed her eyes, then rolled up the shade at the window and sat looking down at the street again.

"That is it—the storm!" she said.

Perhaps, she tried to tell herself, Madame Moonshine *had* listened at the door and now was endeavoring to awaken jealousy in the bosom of Madame Violette, so that she would show Lorenzo Brayton that she was a jealous woman. Most old bachelors, she had understood, had a horror of jealous women.

So she decided that she would be very careful, and ascertain the truth or falsity of Madame Moonshine's statements before indulging in accusations. If Madame Moonshine had spoken the truth, then Lorenzo Brayton was a scoundrel. For, in truth, he had led Madame Violette to believe that she would be his wife one day, and she had listened to his song of approaching prosperity, and had invested in his rubber company almost every cent she possessed about which her son did not know.

She trembled a bit when she considered that perhaps Lorenzo Brayton was a scoundrel and the money lost. In years gone by, before the beauty parlor started her on the road to prosperity, she had saved that money a few cents at a time, put it into a savings bank, and watched the sum total grow. It had been her fond intention to save enough to send her son to college.

But he had told her, on a certain day, that wealth opened doors that knowledge did not, and so he had elected to go to a business school. At the end of the first term he had decided that he had learned all there was to know of business methods. Then he had assumed charge of Madame Violette's business and bank account.

Their ambition was changed. Now they were saving money until the son could have enough to open a broker's office and take a chance at the market. They had discussed it much, and it had become their goal in life. Madame Violette did not know the extent of the bank account as handled by her son, but she felt that it was growing substantially; and she looked forward to the day when she could sell out the beauty parlor and live in luxury.

Lorenzo Brayton had been a prospect, too. Madame Violette was ready to become his wife, not only because of his money and agreeable disposition, but also because she felt that her position would be more secure as a married woman. She did not anticipate reaching the heights in society, but she did wish fervently to predominate in a little corner of her own and make certain of her friends of old days envious.

"That cat was playing a game—and I saw through it!" Madame Violette assured herself now. "It is well that I have found her out. I do not need her friendship!"

She glanced into the mirror again and saw that traces of tears still remained on her cheeks. So she bathed her face and eyes again, and then resorted to her make-up table. Within a few minutes the artificial smile was on her face once more, and she even was humming a tune. She was forcing herself to be the optimistic Madame Violette her patrons knew.

And then came her son, whom she called Raoul.

His entrance was timid, in a way, but Madame Violette did not notice that. She went toward him, smiling, and pressed a peck of a kiss against one of his cheeks. Madame Violette was foolish where her son was concerned.

"It is early," she commented.

"Oh, there's nothing doing to-day, so I came home," Raoul replied.

"And what is this look in your face?" Madame Violette continued. "Are you not feeling well?"

"It—it is just the heat," he replied.

"My baby must take better care of himself."

"And you must stop calling me your baby!" he declared. "One of these days you'll forget and call me that before somebody."

"But you are my baby—my little Raoul!"

"Oh, stop it!" he exclaimed. "My name is George

Gray, and you know it! I'm getting mighty sick of all this fake French business!"

"But it brings the trade," Madame Violette observed. "No woman with an ordinary name can charge the prices I charge. Women in general, my son, have the idea that nobody except a French-woman knows how to massage a face or trim a nail or give a hair treatment. But it will not be for long. Soon we will have money enough, and then——"

"And then we'll get out of this!" her son declared.

"Surely! That has been understood for some time," Madame Violette answered. "You shall have your fine office, with mahogany furniture, and enough capital to make a start. You'll be rich in a few months, and we can live uptown and——"

"Oh, I know the plans, mother! Please don't go into them again now," he said.

"You are peevish!" Madame Violette declared. "That is not like my boy. It is the heat, perhaps. You are sure that you feel quite well?"

"I'm all right—just a little off my feed."

She watched as he sat down before the window, tossed his hat to one side, and looked down at the street. Her son was a good-looking young man, and had intelligence and wit. He was the sort of young man who makes good every day in New York or any other great city. But he was at an age where he was likely to make grave mistakes.

Most mothers—doting mothers, even—would have watched him carefully at this stage and shared all his responsibilities, but not Madame Violette! Already she had accepted him as a seasoned business man.

"I have just had a little spat with Madame Moonshine," she told him now.

"I never did like that woman, mother, and I've told you a dozen times to stay away from her."

"And perhaps you were right. I feel sure that she is a deceitful creature," Madame Violette replied.

"What was the row about?"

"No row—just a little disagreement," Madame Violette hastened to say. "Let us forget all about it. Was there anybody in the other room as you came in?"

"A couple of women waiting for service."

"Mr. Brayton was not there?"

"I didn't see him. Maybe he was in one of the booths. It seems to me that he hangs around here a lot. Does he get a manicure every other hour?"

"Perhaps he comes in the hope that he will catch a sight of me," Madame Violette said, smiling at her son.

The boy turned around quickly and looked up at her.

"You'd better keep him away," he said.

"Why, Raoul! I thought that you admired Mr. Brayton and thought him a great business man."

"Maybe he is, and maybe again he isn't!" the boy said. "He isn't attending to his business when he's hanging around here."

"Then you—you object to a gentleman being interested in me?" she asked.

"Are you trying to tell me that you want to get married again?"

"Well, I grow lonely at times," Madame Violette confessed. "And one of these days you will be getting married—and then I'll be more lonely."

"There are a lot of good men in New York. Lorenzo Brayton isn't the only male human in our little village."

"I—I scarcely understand you, Raoul. I thought that you admired him very much. He admires you —he has told me that you are destined to be a great business man."

"He did, did he?"

"He said that you were wise to the ways of business, and that nobody ever would fool you. You had a nose for good investments, he told me."

"I'm obliged to him!" the boy muttered.

"He said that he was willing to help you at any time—give you tips, and all that."

"He'll have to show me that the tips are mighty good, then! I can get along without his tips."

"You speak as though you had taken his advice and had lost money," his mother accused.

"Oh, I—I just don't feel well!" he said. "It is this confounded heat! I want to be left alone."

"Raoul!"

"And I don't want to be called Raoul!"

"Why, I never saw you like this before!" Madame Violette said. "I can't understand you."

"A business man has worries."

"Of course. Has some of your business been going wrong? Anything about the beauty parlor?"

"Nothing for you to bother your head about," he replied. He got up and turned toward her. "It—it is just the heat! And I had to go around and pay a lot of bills."

"I'd wait until it was cooler."

"I wanted to get the discounts—see? Cash in ten days, ten per cent off."

"I—I suppose so." Madame Violette sighed. "No doubt you know what you are doing. I'll be glad when you can open your office and will not have to endure such drudgery."

"It'll be some time yet. It will take a lot of money. The office isn't all—I'll have to have capital to start, too."

"But our profits are getting larger here, surely," Madame Violette said. "So it is only a question of time."

"Oh, the parlor is all right—turns in a lot of good money," he admitted. "Let's stop talking business until it is cooler."

"Mr. Brayton was saying yesterday——"

"Everything that Brayton says isn't an important fact!" her son interrupted.

"Why, son!"

"S-s-sh!"

The door to the beauty parlor had opened again. Madame Violette turned around quickly, to see a girl standing there. Her son turned back toward the window.

"You wished to see me?" Madame Violette asked.

The girl stepped into the room. She was twenty-two, perhaps, and pretty. She was of medium size, and not of the petite variety. Her abundant hair was chestnut, her eyes were brown, her coloring was rich, and the look of independence was in her face.

Madame Violette realized those things at the first glance. The girl had opened the door softly and had stepped into the room almost like a shadow— nothing at all spectacular or noteworthy about her entrance. Madame Violette remembered it long afterward, and it became a favorite saying of hers that great events are ushered into a person's life in a commonplace sort of way.

"I—I am looking for work," the girl said.

Madame Violette adopted her professional smile and bade her caller be seated. The girl looked up at her frankly. Madame Violette noticed now that she was dressed plainly yet in excellent taste, and that there was an atmosphere of refinement about her—and Madame Violette always insisted upon an atmosphere of refinement in the girls she engaged to work for her. "It is good for the business," she often had said.

"You have done such work before? You have references?" she asked the girl.

"I just came to the city—from Chicago," she replied. "My name is Margaret Dranger. I used to live in New York years ago."

"Oh, yes! But I generally have to demand references," Madame Violette declared. "I cannot be too particular, you see. No doubt you are all right, but——"

"I am at Mrs. Murphy's boarding house, two blocks down the street," Margaret Dranger said. "Mrs. Murphy has known me for years, and she advised me to come to your place first. She will be glad to give you a reference over the telephone. She said that she knew you."

"Well, I should say that Mary Murphy does know me! I boarded with her up to a year or so ago, and so did my son. If Mary Murphy says that you are all right I need no further references. Mary Murphy can look through a girl and give you the history of her life. You know the work?"

"I know manicuring and ordinary facial massage," Margaret said. "If you have some special treatments I'll have to learn those, of course."

"All my girls have to learn those. I really need another girl. Regarding wages——"

"Whatever is customary," said Margaret. "Are the tips very good in this building?"

"I don't think that you'll object to the size of them —and I let my girls keep all the tips," Madame Violette said. "I suppose you can smile sweetly on occasion?"

"I—I suppose so."

"A little flirting, you know——"

"Oh, madame!"

"Nothing naughty, of course, my dear girl. Just a little smile for a tired business man, a look from beneath the eyelids, a pressure of the hand now and then—you understand? It is good for the business, and it brings large tips. What do you think, Raoul?"

Madame Violette, her face beaming, turned toward her son. He whirled around to face her.

"Oh, give her a job!" he replied gruffly.

"Raoul is my only child, my baby," Madame Violette explained to the girl. "He is really my manager. He has an uncanny knack of deciding correctly in all things pertaining to business. He is an excellent judge of a person at the first glance—rarely makes a mistake. So I accept you on his judgment, my dear girl. May I call you Margaret now?"

"Of course."

"Very well, Margaret. You may begin this afternoon, if you like, and learn the 'shop,' and where to find things. Tell Mary Murphy that I shall run in and see her one of these days, when it grows a bit cooler. Hot, isn't it?"

"Very," Margaret said.

"I have a feeling that you are going to be one of my best girls. I do hope nobody coaxes you into matrimony about the time you grow accustomed to the place."

"I am quite sure not, madame!"

"Don't tell me! A girl swears she never will marry—and the next thing we find her name in the list of marriage licenses. Come into the other room with me now and I'll assign you a locker and give you a table. The girls are all busy, and it is about time for two of my pet customers to come in. You may handle one of them."

"Thanks, madame."

"And if you happen to get a Mr. Brayton, please remember that he has a tender left thumb."

"If I get Mr. Brayton, madame, I'll be very careful of his sore thumb!" Margaret said.

Raoul had his back turned again, and Madame Violette was leading the way to the door. Neither was watching Margaret Dranger at the moment, else they might have wondered at the expression on her face.

CHAPTER III

IN the locker room Margaret Dranger hung up her hat and coat and donned an apron furnished by Madame Violette, after which she was shown where to get supplies, and introduced to some of the other girls, and made to feel at home.

"And here is a sort of rest room I have fitted up for my girls," Madame Violette said, holding back the curtains at a doorway. "I would rather have them rest here than loiter about the front room. If they are seen unoccupied it gives to the public the intimation that we are not busy."

"I understand, madame."

"I want you to feel at home, my dear girl, since Mary Murphy has vouched for you."

"Now we will go into the front room. I see that all the girls are busy, and we may expect customers. It is time for some of the men to be leaving their offices."

"Most of them are brokers, are they not, like this Mr. Brayton you mentioned?" Margaret asked.

"Many of them are—and there are lawyers and agents, too. Mr. Brayton comes here a great deal with his friend, a Mr. Peter Satchley. He is a broker, too."

"I suppose they are very wealthy?"

"Blessed with the world's goods, no doubt," said Madame Violette, smiling. "Do not smile too sweetly at Mr. Brayton or you may make somebody else jealous."

"Oh! One of the girls?"

"I scarcely think he would look at a young girl," said Madame Violette. "He is not young himself— and he admires a middle-aged woman. I don't mind saying that he is a bit foolish so far as I am concerned."

"Oh, madame! A romance?"

Madame Violette put her hand to her breast as though to still her fluttering heart and attempted a look of maidenly consternation.

"What happens happens," she admitted. "This is between ourselves, of course. There is nothing settled."

"He must be a splendid man."

"An elegant man, my dear girl—a gentleman if there ever was one. And he understands human nature so well. He thinks a lot of Raoul, my son, too."

"If a rich broker like that were to drop just a few words, he could help other persons make money."

"Certainly," Madame Violette assented. "Treat him nicely, and perhaps he will give you a word that will lead to profits. But not too nicely! Do not make me jealous!"

"I shall be very careful, madame."

"You are a little ray of sunshine. I must thank Mary Murphy for sending you to me," Madame Violette said. "And do not forget the tender thumb!"

Madame Violette's concern about Lorenzo Brayton's sore thumb was not necessary for the moment, however, for Brayton was not the first patron to be attended by Margaret Dranger. The hall door opened and a man entered the parlor. He was middle-aged and dressed in a way that seemed to advertise that he was a man of means.

Madame Violette beamed upon him as she advanced; she always was eager to welcome a strange customer and try to make him a regular patron. He bowed to her and stated that he wished to be manicured, and Madame Violette nodded toward Margaret.

She watched the table for a moment, until she was sure that the new girl knew her business, and then retreated to her private parlor and left them alone at the table in the corner, beneath the shaded lamp.

"It is very warm," the newcomer said.

"Very," Margaret acknowledged.

"I am glad to find a place like this in the building," he went on. "I am to take offices here, and hope to see you regularly."

"Thank you."

"My name is Rathway—Morton Rathway."

"Thank you again. I am Margaret Dranger."

"Warm—isn't it?"

"Very," said Margaret.

She glanced up at him and smiled—and reached for his other hand. Rathway bent closer to her across the table and spoke in a lower tone.

"I feel quite proud of myself to be in this building. I am a manufacturer's agent, and I understand that the building houses big men of affairs, financiers, wealthy brokers."

"I believe so."

"A lot of them come in here, I suppose."

"Naturally," Margaret said.

"I've got a line on a few of them. There is Peter Satchley, for instance—handles big deals as most men handle small ones. Talks in millions!"

"I suppose that one gets used to it after a time."

"And this Lorenzo Brayton!"

"Brayton?"

"The broker," he said. "He handles big deals, too, I understand, and helps out poorer folks now and then by telling them what to buy and when to buy it. Not many weathy brokers do that."

"I suppose not."

"I understand that he has been forming a big rubber company—some South American corporation, I believe. Means millions to him, I suppose. If I were in your shoes, know what I'd do?"

"What?" she asked.

"Smile at him and give him an extra good manicure, and make him give me a tip."

"A lot of good that would do me," said Margaret, laughing. "It takes money even after you have the tip."

"I've seen a broker take ten dollars and make it grow into ten thousand inside a year."

"That was wonderful!"

"I suppose Brayton is a friendly chap?"

"I'm sure I don't know," she replied. "I just came to work here. You are my first customer."

"Oh!" Rathway exclaimed.

As he started to go, Madame Violette came into the room again, and he bowed before her.

"I find the service very satisfactory," he said. "Allow me—my name is Rathway—going to have an office in the building. I was just telling Miss— Dranger, wasn't it?—that I'm glad to find such a place so conveniently located. I'm all puffed up, too —having an office in the same building as such men as Satchley and Brayton."

"Oh! You know those gentlemen?"

"By reputation only," Rathway said. "I hope to meet them, though. I have a bit of money to invest when the right investment comes along—legacy left me recently. Want to go in with the right sort of broker, of course."

"Of course!" Madame Violette said.

"I suppose Brayton is all right, for instance?"

"He seems to do a big business," Madame Violette admitted. "I believe that he is very wealthy."

"Nice chap, eh?"

"I have found him a perfect gentleman—so far."

"Have to meet him as soon as possible," Rathway declared. "I'll bet he could make a fortune for a man—or a woman."

"I dare say Mr. Brayton knows a great deal about financial affairs," Madame Violette answered.

"Do you suppose he'd pay any attention to a small investment like mine? I've only three thousand that I can gamble with."

"Of course I do not know, Mr. Rathway," Madame Violette said. "I'd advise that you see him about it. I know of one small sum he handled—four thousand, to be exact."

"Ah! I see! Perhaps there is hope for me, then. And again—perhaps he handled that investment just to please a lady?"

Madame Violette pretended a blush and turned away, simulating confusion.

"Pardon me," Rathway said. "I didn't want to pry into private matters, of course. I hope to be a regular customer here. Good afternoon, Miss Dranger. And you—Madame Violette, is it not?"

He bowed before them, whirled on his heel, passed through the door, and closed it softly after him as though it had been the door of a sick room.

"A splendid man, so he seems," Madame Violette said.

"An inquisitive one," Margaret Dranger added.

"My dear girl!"

"He was trying to pump me about Mr. Satchley and Mr. Brayton, and he was disappointed when I told him I had just come here and did not know the gentlemen. And he was trying to pump you, too, Madame Violette."

"The very idea!"

"But probably it was because he wanted to know all about the man he intrusted with his money."

"I suppose that was the reason," Madame Violette said.

She walked back toward the booths, and for the second time that afternoon she failed to see a peculiar look in Margaret Dranger's face.

CHAPTER IV

CROOKS DISAGREE

PETER SATCHLEY glanced up from his desk as his stenographer put some letters before him.

"That will be all for to-day," he said. "Go some place and try to be cool. This is terrible weather. Tell that imp in the front office to clear out, too."

Having thus dismissed the stenographer and office boy, Peter Satchley got up and went to the water cooler in a corner of his private office, took a drink, and then remained standing by a window looking down into the court of the building. Before his eyes were scores of open windows, and inside them stenographers and business men were sitting, but Peter Satchley did not see these busy human beings. He was thinking.

After a time he turned back to his desk again, sat down before it, and perused for the hundredth time a paper upon it—the confidential report made him that day by a certain commercial agency. He smote the desk with his fist and made the ink bottles jump.

"After all these years!" he exclaimed. "Caught by one of my own kind, and in my own sort of game. I'll take it out of his hide if he doesn't come through! I'll——"

He realized that he was voicing a threat aloud, and

got up quickly and hurried to the door. He was relieved to find that there was nobody in the outer
office.

"I'll see him right now—won't wait another minute!" Satchley told himself.

He closed his desk, got his hat, went into the
corridor, and locked the door behind him. He hurried to the stairs, and went down one flight angrily,
and along the corridor on the floor below, his anger
increasing at every step. But as he reached the offices
of Lorenzo Brayton he fought to control himself.
Brayton could read a man's face, and Satchley wanted
to play the game in the correct manner. He wanted
to catch Lorenzo Brayton off guard.

Brayton's stenographer nodded when Satchley entered the office, and indicated by a single toss of
her head that Brayton was in and that Satchley
was free to go into the private room. Satchley
found Brayton sitting before his desk adding long
columns of figures.

"I've sent my girl home to cool off," Satchley
said. "Why not follow my example?"

He grinned as he spoke, and Lorenzo Brayton
glanced up at him and closed his left eye in a
deliberate wink.

"Excellent idea, Satchley," he said; and he went
into the other room and released the stenographer.
She lost no time in getting out of the office.

Satchley had seated himself at one end of the
desk.

"What's on your mind?" Brayton asked, sitting
before the desk again. "Got a line on a sucker

with coin? Want to place a little block of rubber stock?"

"I just wanted to talk—communion of kindred spirits, and all that."

"Well, talk," Brayton said. "Our conversations generally result in some good scheme."

"We've formulated many a good scheme," Satchley told him. "Let me see—it's been almost fifteen years since we met, hasn't it?"

"Just about."

"Out in San Francisco, wasn't it? I saw you pick a man's pocket, and when he raised a howl I gave you the high sign and you slipped the wallet to me, and I got away with it while you pretended righteous indignation."

"I was scared for a minute."

"We were pikers, then," Satchley said. "Common dips! But we improved."

"I'll say that we did!"

"We got our brain working together and evolved as pretty a swindle as ever was perpetrated. We gathered in some coin and moved on to New Orleans. Handled a bit of everything, didn't we?"

"We did. Remember how we worked the old race-track game in El Paso?"

"I do. But we soon graduated from the old games," said Satchley. "And we got the idea that we'd be lucky as long as we held together, didn't we?"

"And haven't we been?"

"We certainly have made some money," Satchley admitted.

"But why discuss ancient history in such hot weather?" Brayton asked.

"I just wondered if, in your prosperity, you remembered how we have worked up together. We swore eternal friendship about ten or twelve years ago, I believe."

"We certainly did," Brayton admitted.

"A pretty thing—friendship between men! What was mine was to be yours, and what was yours was to be mine if needed."

"Sure!" said Brayton.

"We agreed to stand by each other in everything."

"Well, we've done it, I guess! I've helped you and you've helped me. And this double-office game is a winner. We can send the sheep to each other and shear them right!"

"We're all right as long as we confine ourselves to sheep and don't bother the goats."

"What's the meaning of that deep remark?" Brayton asked.

"If a man has been a roaring lion for a few years —or thinks he has been—it hurts his dignity to find out that he is only a goat. It also injures his pocketbook."

"You grow poetical," Brayton said, chuckling. "Have you seen some lion turning into a goat?"

Peter Satchley tossed the end of his cigar into the nearest cuspidor and looked across at Brayton with a new expression in his countenance.

"Brayton," he said, "the time has come for a show-down."

"Explain yourself, my friend."

"Be careful with that word 'friend,' Brayton. It is a word that's misused a lot."

"I don't seem to gather your meaning."

Peter Satchley bent forward across the end of the desk. His eyes suddenly blazed.

"You had a nerve to try it on me!" he exclaimed.

"Are you insane, Pete—sick with the heat?"

"It won't do you any good to try to be clever with me, Brayton! I can read you as easily as I can the newspaper I get at the door every morning. I'm wise! You—dirty—crook!"

"The pot calls the kettle black, I observe."

"Oh, I'm a crook, and I admit it as far as you are concerned. I'm a crook—and I've always been a crook! I'm a high-class swindler—but a crook, nevertheless. But I'm a decent crook, curse you!"

"I don't get this," Brayton said.

"You get it, all right. There's supposed to be honor among thieves, but you seem to forget it. Or maybe you don't know what honor means. Brayton, for almost fifteen years we've worked together. We've been in danger, and we've played safe. We've been poor and we've been rich—put up at the best hotels, and run a bluff to get a square meal. So we should be pals."

"Well?"

"And you—you crook!—turn against a friendship like that. For a measly ten thousand dollars you smash everything. I've just found out about that holding-company gag of yours. I've had a report from an honest agency, something we don't deal with often. I was a little suspicious, but I wouldn't even believe that report until I had verified it by another. You've swindled me—your old partner— you old crook partner!"

"You must be insane!"

"Don't tell me that again!" Satchley cried. "I'm really sane for the first time in years, since I cease to trust you. Couldn't keep your fingers off my ten thousand, could you? I suppose there weren't suckers enough in town—you had to rob your partner. Brayton you're about as low as a human can become."

"I don't fancy that line of talk!" Brayton retorted.

"As though I cared! You'll listen to it, all right! Wreck a partnership like ours for ten thousand, will you?"

"It was just a joke, you ass! Just a little trick to wake you up and put you on your mettle; I was afraid you were growing careless because of our prosperity."

"A joke, was it? Don't lie to me, Brayton. You nicked me for ten thousand, and you meant to keep the coin. Don't forget that I had a report from a commercial agency, and it covers the entire deal. If it had been a joke you wouldn't have gone to so much trouble to hide your fine Italian hand in the business. You're a crooked crook, Brayton— and a liar as well!"

"Satchley, I don't intend to stand for much more of this, even if we have been together for fifteen years."

"What else can you do?" Peter Satchley sneered. "You've smashed everything! I'm done with you, Brayton. Go it alone—and see how far you get. You can throw a bluff, but I'm the brains of the combination, and you know it. You'll be pinched before you're a month older—and you'll do time, too! Go it alone—you crook! You couldn't keep your fingers off that ten thousand, though it belonged to your partner. Well, that ten thousand will cost you something!"

"I don't care to hear any more of your threats."

"I'm not making threats—I'm giving you a plain statement of facts," Satchley declared. "No man can do to me what you've done and get away with it!"

"That so?" Lorenzo Brayton said, sneering and getting quickly out of his desk chair. "Well, let me tell you something, Satchley! I don't need you any longer. I can get along just as well, or better, alone, and keep from splitting the profits. Put that into your pipe and smoke it!"

"You can, eh?"

"I can! And if it's revenge you're after, you'll not get it by running to the police with a story. You have me pulled, and you will be in the next cell. Don't forget that!"

Now Satchley sprang to his feet, too, his face livid with rage, and lurched forward to wave a clenched fist beneath the nose of Lorenzo Brayton.

"Don't you dare intimate that I'd do such a thing!" he cried. "I may be a crook, but I'm a decent one. I'll not turn you up to the police—but

I'll be square with you, all right!   I'll take that ten thousand out of your hide!"

An oath escaped the lips of Lorenzo Brayton. He took another step, his fist swung up and was launched forward.   But Peter Satchley had been anticipating that.   He stepped quickly and neatly to one side and dodged the blow, and his own right fist caught Lorenzo Brayton on the side of the head and staggered him.

Brayton cursed and charged again.   Once more Satchley sidestepped, and this time he put the entire weight of his body behind the blow he delivered.   His aim was true, too—his fist crashed against the point of Lorenzo Brayton's chin.

Brayton swayed, his eyes closed, a spasm of agony flashed across his countenance, and then he collapsed to the floor.

"And there's more coming, you crook!" Satchley shouted.   He did not even glance at his fallen foe. He darted through the outer office and into the corridor, almost colliding with a man in front of the door.   The man was Mr. Morton Rathway.

Satchley hurried up the stairs and to his own office, his anger consuming him.   Rathway waited until he had disappeared, and then darted into Brayton's office and closed the door.   He hastened to the private office.   Lorenzo Brayton was still unconscious on the floor.

"That was some smash!" Rathway told himself. "Everything dropping right into my hands.   Lucky I happened to hear their voices and took a look through the keyhole.   Well—to work!"

He knelt beside the unconscious man, and his hands explored the pockets of Lorenzo Brayton swiftly and with skill. Out came a bunch of keys; Rathway looked them over, selected two, and made impressions of them on tiny tablets of wax that he took from one of his pockets.

Making sure that Brayton was still unconscious, Rathway put a hand into the fallen man's waistcoat pocket and extracted a little memorandum book. He turned the pages swiftly until he came to one that had a combination written upon it, then took a book from his own pocket, copied the combination, and returned Rathway's book.

"So!" he mused, grinning. "Easy! Thanks to Mr. Peter Satchley! I'll have to remember his kindness when the proper time comes."

Now Rathway sprang to his feet, hurried through the outer office, and dashed into the hall. Down it shuffled an old janitor. Rathway called to him.

"Trouble in here!" he exclaimed. "I'm Rathway —opening a new office on the tenth floor. Came in to see Mr. Brayton about some investments. He's on the floor, unconscious—looks as though there had been a fight!"

The old janitor led the way into the room. Brayton was moaning now, and while the janitor raised his head Rathway hurried to the water cooler in the corner and returned with a glass of water. He dashed it into Brayton's face, filled the glass again, and returned to hold it to Brayton's lips.

Brayton moaned again—and opened his eyes.

"What has happened?" the old janitor asked.

"What was it, Mr. Brayton? This is old Frand speaking. Don't you know Frand, the janitor? Was it a thief? Quick, Mr. Brayton!"

Brayton struggled to sit up, and they helped him to a chair.

"It's—it's nothing," Brayton muttered. "The heat. I fainted, I guess. I must have fallen—and struck my head."

"This gentleman came in and found you," Frand said. "He called to me. I was afraid you had been attacked."

"Just the heat. I fell."

Morton Rathway, going for more water, smiled grimly.

"Shall I call a doctor, Mr. Brayton—or order a taxi?" Frand asked.

"No. I'm all right now, Frand. I've been eating rich food—and not taking enough exercise—working too hard."

"You're sure that you're all right, sir?"

"Yes, I'm all right. Sorry to make such a nuisance of myself."

"If I can do anything——" Frand began.

"Nothing at all. Thanks for what you have done."

"I—I'd hate to have anything happen to you, sir—just now."

"I understand," Brayton said, looking up at the old janitor and smiling. "Don't you worry, Frand. I'm all right. I'll be as fresh as a youngster by morning."

Frand left him and went toward the door. There

he turned, but Lorenzo Brayton already was himself again and waved for the old janitor to proceed. Frand went out, and Brayton looked toward Rathway.

"You found me?" he asked.

"Yes, sir. My name's Rathway—opening an office on the tenth floor—manufacturer's agent. I've got a bit of money left me and want to invest it. I was coming in to see if you had anything to offer. Found you on the floor."

"Er—nobody else around?" Brayton asked.

"No, sir. I saw a gentleman going along the hall, but didn't notice him particularly. You must have had a nasty fall."

"Dizzy spell," Brayton explained.

"Are you subject to such spells?" Rathway asked maliciously.

"No—it's the heat. Regarding your business, can you call to-morrow or the day following? I don't feel like talking business just now."

"Then I'll call later," Rathway said. "Sure you're all right? Don't want me to call a physician, or anything like that?"

"No, thanks."

"I'll see you later, then. Good afternoon!"

CHAPTER V

LEFT alone, Lorenzo Brayton sat before his mahogany desk and pondered over what had occurred. He felt of his sore jaw and registered a vow to square matters with Peter Satchley one day. No idea of having Satchley arrested for simple assault entered his mind. This was not a case for a man to resort to an ordinary arrest and a trial before a police magistrate.

Brayton was a bit chagrined, too, because he experienced a feeling of having been found out. He had thought that he had swindled his old partner cleverly, and had not taken into account that Satchley was clever, too, and might grow suspicious even of Lorenzo Brayton, despite their years of working together.

He was a bit afraid of Peter Satchley. He knew, of course, that Satchley would not betray their past dealings, since he was involved as deeply as Brayton; Peter Satchley was not the sort of man to go to jail himself just in order to send an enemy there. But Brayton did not doubt that Satchley would strike again in the future, and in some clever manner. He would have to be on guard always.

He got up after a time and went to the mirror

over the washstand in the corner and looked at the reflection of his countenance there. Satchley's first blow had struck him on the side of the head, and its results, consisting of a small lump beneath Brayton's ample hair, could not be observed easily. But the second and last blow had struck him squarely on the point of the jaw, and Brayton found that his chin was swollen slightly and discolored a bit.

He bathed the chin in cold water, bathed his head also, and returned to his desk. His chaotic anger had given place to a cool determination to square accounts with Peter Satchley as soon as possible, and in such a manner that Satchley would be convinced that Lorenzo Brayton was the better man. But Brayton decided to drop all thought of it for the time being; he wanted to wait until he was sure that his anger had cooled, and then formulate some plan that would be without a flaw.

To get his mind off the recent brawl, he inspected a mass of papers on his desk, filed some of them, and glanced through the financial columns of the early edition of his favorite evening paper. He thought of the man who had called himself Rathway and had said that he wanted to make an investment, and smiled. Lorenzo Brayton always was glad to meet a man looking for an investment.

"I don't need Satchley any more!" he declared to himself. "I haven't needed him for some time. I'm plenty big enough to stand alone now—and what's the sense in splitting the profits?"

He glanced at his watch and discovered that it was after four o'clock. Closing his desk, he put on his hat, glanced around the office, and went toward the corridor.

He did not have to wait long for the elevator, and when it stopped to pick him up Brayton found that in it were a couple of men with whom he was acquainted. They spoke to him and continued the conversation until the elevator reached the ground floor, and Brayton saw with satisfaction that neither seemed to notice the slight swelling and discoloration of his chin.

In the lobby of the building he stopped for a moment at the news stand to purchase some cigars.

"Isn't this Mr. Brayton?" asked a voice behind him.

Brayton turned, a smile on his face and a hand ready to clasp another. His smile was part of his stock in trade, the same as Madame Violette's. Before him was a giant of a man with clear, piercing eyes.

"Sam Haynes!" Brayton gasped.

"The same!"

"Still working in the police department?"

"Sure," Haynes replied. "Life job, you know, if I don't make any slips. I didn't know you were in this building."

"Been here four or five months," Brayton replied. "Offices on the fifth floor. Drop in and see me some time."

"Sure," Haynes said.

"Working nights now? I see you're not in uniform."

"I'm in the detective department now, Mr. Brayton—promoted four months ago for a bit of work I did."

"Good enough! Making them open their eyes, are you?"

"Oh, I'm getting along all right," Detective Sam Haynes said.

"Makes me nervous to be talking to a detective," Brayton said, laughing a bit. "Especially when he is hanging around my building and as good as puts a hand on my shoulder. Not after me or any of my friends, are you?"

"If I'm ever interested unduly in you, Mr. Brayton, it'll be because you're the victim of foul play or a candidate for the electric chair. I'm in the homicide squad," Detective Sam Haynes said.

Brayton pretended to shiver. "Here's hoping, then, that we meet on a friendship basis only," he replied. "Interesting work, I suppose—but gruesome!"

"Interesting is the correct word," Haynes said. "Do you know, some of the old men on the squad declare that they can feel a murder coming? Last week one of the boys got to hanging around a block downtown—common block of no importance—and couldn't explain to himself or to us why he did it. Well, he felt a murder. That was the block where we found the body of that Philadelphia girl who had been missing for a couple of weeks."

"Great Scott!" Brayton gasped. "Can *you* feel 'em coming, too? And you're hanging around this building!"

"And there are several hundred persons in this

building, so you need not worry," Haynes told him. "As a matter of fact, I dropped in here to see a dentist. I felt like homicide by the time he had finished with me, but I held my hand. And this is homicide weather, too. Stagnant, hot weather like this always increases the percentage of murders and suicides. Men go wild and jump on their best friends."

"I—I've noticed that," Brayton said.

"I think there's going to be a big storm."

"Everybody is saying that," Brayton declared.

"Well, I must be getting back to headquarters. Glad to have met you again, Brayton. I'll drop in and see you the first time I have some coin I want to double."

"Do, Haynes—do!" Brayton said. "I'll find something nice and profitable for you. But I hope you'll never—er—drop in professionally."

"Hope so, too," Detective Sam Haynes said.

He went on toward the street, and Brayton turned around to light his cigar, and then followed slowly. He had met Sam Haynes a year before, when he had been an important witness in an accident case, and had taken a liking to the officer. He knew that Haynes had native intelligence and cleverness and would go far.

"Hate to have him on my trail," Brayton said to himself. "So weather like this often makes men jump on their best friends, does it? Well, Pete Satchley needn't bring that fact to me as an alibi for what he's done. I'll smash Pete Satchley if it takes me ten years!"

At the entrance he met Frand, the old janitor, again.

"Feeling quite well now, sir?" Frand asked in his thin, quavering voice.

"I'm all right, Frand," Brayton replied.

"I think it is growing a bit cooler, sir—I hope so. They tell me that several yound ladies in the building were sent home ill to-day because of the heat. Shall I call a taxi for you, sir?"

"Don't bother, Frand."

"I'm very glad that you are all right again, sir, and hope you will be yourself to-morrow. I was a bit frightened when the gentleman called me and we found you unconscious on the floor."

"Just a faint."

"But it was so like my dream, sir."

"Dream?" Brayton asked.

"Yes, sir. I was dreaming last night, sir—about you."

"Well, that is interesting."

"And I woke in a fright, sir, with the perspiration standing out on my face. I—I thought that you had been murdered, sir."

"For Heaven's sake!" Brayton gasped.

"I could see you plainly, sir, stretched out on the floor in your private office—just as you were found this afternoon—and you had been shot, sir. You were quite dead, and the detectives were trying to solve the mystery. It certainly gave me a fright, sir—you know why."

"I beg your pardon?"

"If anything were to happen to you, sir——"

"Nothing is going to happen to me!" Lorenzo Brayton declared. "It is said that dreams go by contraries. There is nothing to dreams, anyway."

"Our—our little affair, sir—it is all right?"

Brayton looked down at the old man's anxious face and smiled reassuringly.

"You can bet it is all right," he answered in a lower tone. "Don't you worry a bit, Frand."

"Thanks, sir. Well—good afternoon, Mr. Brayton! Feels like a storm, doesn't it?"

Brayton stepped out of the building without making a reply. Why did every fool in town, he wondered, talk about storms and violence, murders and shootings?

"Gets on a man's nerves!" Lorenzo Brayton told himself.

He turned into a haberdasher's shop on the ground floor of the building. It was a small but profitable shop. The two clerks were busy in the rear, and the proprietor, a George Brown, hurried forward with a smile when Brayton entered.

"Half a dozen pairs of socks—the usual sort, Brown," Brayton said.

"Right here, sir!" Brown replied. "Hot, isn't it?"

"Yes. Now don't say that you think there is going to be a storm. Everybody seems to be saying something like that this afternoon."

"As a matter of fact, Mr. Brayton, it was on the tip of my tongue to say just that."

"I knew it! Human minds seem to run in the same channel on a day like this."

Brown looked at him in a peculiar fashion.

"Everything all right?" he asked in a low tone.

"Quite!" Brayton said.

"Our—our little deal——"

"Couldn't be better," Brayton said.

"I'm certainly glad of that. If anything was to go wrong—— But nothing will go wrong, of course."

"That's the way to look at it, Brown. Just forget it and leave it to me. That's my business, you know. You don't suppose I'd let things go wrong, do you? Haven't you confidence in me?"

"Certainly, sir."

"Very well, then," Brayton said.

"I grow enthusiastic at times, and I worry a bit at times, but that is only natural, I suppose," Brown told him. "It's—it's something new for me, you understand."

"Of course."

"And it means so much to me! Look here, sir— new garters! See how flexible they are. Rubber!"

"Ah!" Brayton said winking.

"See these suspenders? Rubber!"

"Ah! Yes!"

"See those automobile tires out there in the street? Rubber! See the insulation on those wires? Millions and millions of miles of wire like that! All rubber!"

"You've a wise head, Brown, and a good pair of eyes," Brayton said, flattering him.

"And I keep telling myself that everything is coming out all right."

"Certainly! You're not forgetting about keeping quiet?"

"No, sir. Nobody can get a word out of me, Mr. Brayton!"

"That's the boy. If anything can spoil our plans it is a foolish word dropped carelessly."

"I'll not be the one to drop it!" Brown declared. "You may depend upon me, sir!"

"I'm sure of it," Brayton said, taking the package of socks and handing Brown a bill.

"And nobody else better drop it, either!" Brown said in a tense voice. "You know what it means to me, Mr. Brayton—I explained that to you fully at the time. I'd go insane, I believe, if things went wrong. I—I'd kill——"

"For Heaven's sake!" Brayton gasped. "Everybody to-day is talking of murder. I supposed that you had a certain amount of nerve, Brown, or I never would have approached you in the matter. I presume it is because it is new to you."

"And because it means so much," Brown added. "And then I have heard, of course, of such things going wrong. But generally it was because somebody was crooked."

"You don't think that I'd be crooked?" Brayton asked.

"You'd better not prove to be!" the haberdasher said. "If you were, Mr. Brayton, I'd probably choke the life out of you—and, if I wasn't able to do that, I'd probably get me an automatic and indulge in a little target practice—with you for the target! But that is only wild talk, of course."

"It certainly is wild," Brayton said. "The heat

is having its effect on your brain. Take a grip on yourself, Brown!"

Brayton turned to leave the establishment. He almost collided with Morton Rathway, who stepped aside with a grin and an apology and then asked Brown whether he had some purple socks in stock.

As Brown sought the socks, Morton Rathway looked after the disappearing Brayton. Rathway's eyes had narrowed, and the grin had left his face!

CHAPTER VI

THAT afternoon Madame Violette waited in vain for Lorenzo Brayton to come into her establishment. She wanted to talk to him and convince herself that Madame Moonshine was a meddling woman and that the truth was not in her, and that Brayton still remained a captive to her own charms.

But Brayton had gone to his apartment on Riverside Drive, had abused his Japanese boy of all work roundly for no particular reason, had given him a bill of generous denomination to buy salve for his wounded feelings, and then had sulked in his den until time to retire.

In the morning, however, Lorenzo Brayton was his smiling self again, and save for a soreness at the point of the jaw the one-sided combat with Peter Satchley might not have occurred. The evening before Brayton had felt a sort of premonition and had been depressed in spirit, but the feeling had disappeared during the night.

He reached his office at the usual hour, greeted the office boy and stenographer jovially, and attacked a mass of mail that he found on his desk. For an hour he disposed of orders for stock, dictated several replies, arranged for the payment of current bills, and then began the perusal of letters that had been tossed to one side as personal.

Brayton put in a busy morning. The luncheon hour came almost before he was aware of it. It brought another thought of Peter Satchley. It had been the custom for Brayton to take lunch with Satchley every day at a restaurant around the corner. To-day Brayton was doomed to go out alone.

In the lobby of the building he bumped into Detective Sam Haynes again.

"You still hanging around this building?" Brayton asked. "Feel a murder, like you said that other detective did? Sharks following the ship, eh?"

Detective Sam Haynes laughed as he held a flaming match to a cigar.

"I really don't know why I'm here," he confessed. "I was walking down the street and just dropped into the lobby to get a cigar. Can't understand why I didn't patronize my favorite cigar store on the corner below. Now that you mention it, Mr. Brayton, it does seem peculiar."

"Hope there isn't any violence," Brayton said. "I don't want to be—er—a subject for the medical examiner or a candidate for the electric chair."

"Hope you'll be neither," said Haynes. "What's the matter with your chin?"

"Chin?" Brayton asked in alarm.

"Bruised," Haynes said.

"Oh! Didn't know anybody could see it. I fainted yesterday afternoon because of the heat, fell in my private office, and struck my chin against the corner of the desk."

"Um!" Haynes grunted. "If you hadn't told me,

Mr. Brayton, I'd have sworn that somebody had landed a knockout blow on your jaw. I've seen a lot of them in my time, and that is the way your face certainly looks."

"Nonsense! But it was a knockout, all right," Brayton replied. "You'll have to excuse me now— I've got to hurry to lunch."

He did hurry, and Detective Sam Haynes looked after him in a speculative manner.

"He can't tell me!" Haynes mused. "It isn't only that chin, either—but the way he acted. Somebody put over a haymaker on Mr. Lorenzo Brayton!"

Brayton had been a little disconcerted by Haynes' statement, but told himself that nobody else would notice the swollen chin. He entered the restaurant and found Peter Satchley already at the table they generally used. Satchley grinned maliciously and Brayton went to another table, an act many men in the café noticed.

He ate leisurely, giving Satchley a chance to leave the place before him; and then he walked down the street a few blocks and finally turned back toward the office building. But he did not enter the elevator and ascend to his office. He went toward the establishment of Madame Moonshine, modiste.

At that hour, Madame Moonshine was not bothered with patrons, and when Lorenzo Brayton entered the shop she went forward to meet him, her face beaming, while her saleswomen and models glanced at one another and smiled in a knowing manner.

"Come right into my office, Mr. Brayton," she called. "I have those papers ready for you."

Madame Moonshine fondly believed that this was subterfuge, that her saleswomen and models would think she had business dealings with Lorenzo Brayton and no further interest in him—and her employees let her so believe.

She ushered Brayton into her private office, chatting cordially the while, closed the door, and then whirled to face him, concern in her countenance.

"Why did you not tell me?" she asked. "Why did you not send for me?"

"I beg your pardon?"

"Oh, Frand has told me all about it—how you became ill in your office because of the heat yesterday afternoon, and how you fainted. My dear Lorenzo, it frightened me dreadfully! Suppose you had injured yourself!"

"It was only a bump on the chin," Brayton replied cheerfully. "I wanted nobody to learn of it. It seemed such a childish thing to do."

"You have seen a physician?"

"No. It was nothing—just the heat, and perhaps a slight attack of indigestion. It was nothing, Madame Moonshine."

"Call me Hortense," she begged, smiling at him. "I wondered why I did not see you yesterday evening. But I am very glad to see you now, my dear Lorenzo. I—I wanted to speak to you about something yesterday."

"Why not speak of it now?"

"It—it is rather a delicate subject, my dear Lorenzo," Madame Moonshine said, plucking at the sleeve of his coat and glancing away coyly. "Lorenzo, I am desperately afriad that our little romance has been discovered."

"Really?" Brayton gasped.

"And by that dreadful Madame Violette, who runs that beauty parlor upstairs."

"Dreadful Madame Violette? I thought that she was your particular friend?"

"Oo, la! I believed so myself until yesterday afternoon. The spy!"

"Spy?"

"What else?" Madame Moonshine demanded hotly. "I dropped in to see her, and she was gazing into that foolish crystal of hers as though she believed in the thing. She said that there was going to be a great storm."

"Everybody was saying so yesterday."

"But she told me that it was only a symbol—that by a storm she meant serious trouble. She spoke a lot concerning swirling clouds and that sort of thing. Oo, la, la! And then it came out. We got to speaking of you, my dear Lorenzo."

"Nothing bad, I hope."

"Lorenzo, that woman must have been watching us. Just consider it! She spoke of sly kisses, and tips regarding investments, and then attempted to make me believe that you were interested in her and were about to ask her to be your wife. That was ridiculous, of course."

"Of course!" Brayton assented.

"I—I should hate to have talk get about, Lorenzo."

She let go his sleeve and dabbed at her eyes with a bit of lace she used for a handkerchief. Lorenzo Brayton regarded her for a moment, and then stepped forward and put an arm around her, and she looked up and smiled.

"We must not let the talk get out, that is true," he said. "There is your reputation to be considered."

"Oh, Lorenzo!"

"My dear Hortense, I am truly sorry that such a thing happened. I am sure that you have understood my feelings correctly. I intend to ask you to become my wife. But I would rather wait until this big deal of mine is consummated, and it will not be long now. Can we not just have a friendly understanding between us? Then, when you encounter such a woman as this Madame Violette, you can smile and tell yourself that she does not know everything."

"Oh, Lorenzo!" Madame Moonshine gushed.

She lifted her head, and Brayton bent his and touched her lips with his own.

"I am so happy!" she said.

"Not nearly so happy as I am," Brayton declared. "But it is to be our secret for the present, remember. A man cannot attend to big business and to love at the same time without neglecting the one or the other. We must stifle our affection, my dear Hortense, until I have accomplished my purpose. And then we shall take a long honeymoon, and, best of all, we shall have plenty of gold to spend."

"Oh, my dear Lorenzo! Such a secret for a woman to keep locked up in her heart!"

"And can you keep it, or are you like the women they say cannot refrain from telling?"

"Hortense Moonshine can keep a secret—especially in such a case as this," she declared.

For that, Lorenzo Brayton kissed her again as she cuddled against him. And then he sat down on a divan with the doting Madame Moonshine by his side.

"Everything is going well," he reported, assuming the voice of a business man. "If you care to invest more——"

"I can spare two hundred to-day, Lorenzo. I should use it to pay a bill, but the bill can wait a week."

"Very good! Get me the money, and I'll send the stock certificate down to you this afternoon by my stenographer. That closes the stock issue except for one hundred dollars more, and I already have promised that."

"It is good that I can trust you, Lorenzo. I could not afford such a loss. The earnings of years——"

"Do you not trust me?"

"Of course!" she breathed. "You are not a scoundrel. Do you know, my dear Lorenzo, what Hortense Moonshine would do to a man that swindled her of money or made mock of her love? That man would die the death, Lorenzo! But I can trust you, of course!"

Brayton cleared his throat and adopted the professional tone once more.

"I expected to call a meeting of the stockholders within a week," he said. "And I shall insist that you be elected second vice president of the company."

"Oh, Lorenzo!"

"And there is no doubt that I can make a deal with a certain big corporation that will double the value of our investments and at the same time leave us stock that will pay huge dividends."

"Then there will be no need of busy office hours for you in the future," she said. "We can live easily, travel where we please—just love each other, Lorenzo."

"Exactly, my dear Hortense," he replied. "And now I must get back to the office. And I think that it would be better if we did not see so much of each other for a week or so. We do not want tongues to wag, my dear girl. I do not want persons speaking lightly of my future wife. We'll keep our little secret until after the meeting of the stockholders, eh?"

"Yes, dear Lorenzo!"

Madame Moonshine held up her head again, and once more he kissed her, and then they walked toward the door.

"Oh, by the way—the two hundred!" Lorenzo reminded her gently.

Madame Moonshine, her face beaming, hurried to her desk and returned with a roll of bills which she handed to Brayton. He slipped them into his coat pocket as though they had been so much waste paper.

"I'll send the stock certificate down to you this afternoon, my dear Hortense," he said.

CHAPTER VII

TROUBLE BREWING

THE more Peter Satchley thought of his ten thousand dollars that had gone into the pockets of Lorenzo Brayton the angrier he became. He had assuaged his rage to a certain extent by smashing Brayton on the point of the chin and rendering him unconscious, but that was only a first installment of his vengeance.

Catching sight of Brayton in the restaurant during the luncheon hour had added fuel to the flames of Peter Satchley's wrath. He returned to his office and sat before the desk, telling his stenographer and office boy that he was not to be disturbed for the time being, and began considering methods of making Brayton pay. He had no idea of regaining the ten thousand; he knew from past experiences that when Brayton got his clutches on money that money was lost forever to the rightful owner.

There had been certain shady deals in which Satchley and Brayton had enjoyed a silent partnership and divided the illicit profits. But Brayton, as Satchley knew very well, had branched out and constructed some shady deals of his own, forgetting to let his partner have a share of the proceeds.

The holding company that had cost Satchley ten thousand dollars was one of these—and there were others about which Satchley knew. The confidential report of the commercial agency had served to open Peter Satchley's eyes.

"Swindle me, will he?" Satchley said to himself. "Well, I'll make him pay for it!"

Having been close to Lorenzo Brayton for almost fifteen years, Satchley knew his methods well. Moreover, Brayton had spoken to him of certain "prospects" and "suckers" and "easy marks." Sitting before his desk and thinking of these things, Satchley evolved a plan for causing Brayton annoyance at least, and possibly deep trouble.

He put on his hat and left the office, telling the stenographer that he would not return until late, and possibly not at all that afternoon. Down in the elevator he went and out upon the street. He signaled for a taxicab and drove to a brokerage office patronized extensively by those of the district, mainly would-be financiers.

Satchley had been in the place many times before, always giving the impression that he disapproved of such things and went there only on the possibility of picking up a few scattered shares of stock for some customer. He nodded to the floor manager and glanced at the huge blackboard and the quotations there.

He allowed his eyes to roam around the room until he spotted the man he sought, and then he made his way slowly and cautiously through the crowd until he reached this man's side.

"And how is the young financier?" Satchley asked in a low voice, smiling benevolently.

The other turned to face him. It was Madame Violette's son.

"Hello, Mr. Satchley!" he said, proud of the fact that the broker had singled him out of the crowd and had spoken to him first. "I'm all right, thanks. Just watching the market a bit."

"Not dabbling any?"

"Not to-day."

"Sneak outside," Satchley said, lowering his voice, "and walk to the end of the corridor. I'll follow you in a minute or so. I've got something important to tell you—valuable information I think you'll thank me for giving you."

Satchley turned away and struggled to get nearer the blackboards. He watched until Madame Violette's son had left the room, and then he followed, and found his man at the end of the corridor looking through the window at the street.

"Raoul——" he began.

"Pardon me, Mr. Satchley. My right name is George Gray—that Raoul stuff is only for the beauty parlor."

"Ah, yes! Very well, George. I have been watching you for some time, and you impress me as a wise young man. But, if you'll pardon me, you're just at an age when it is easy to make mistakes. I overestimated myself when I was about your age, and it cost me a great deal."

"Sorry!" the boy said.

"I am inclined to the belief that you are being victimized. What I am to say to you must go no further."

"You may depend upon me, Mr. Satchley."

"Very well. I have your word of honor?"

The boy nodded.

"I know a great deal about Lorenzo Brayton," Satchley said, talking in a low tone and making sure that nobody else was near. "I have known him for many years, and I have just discovered that he is a scoundrel. We have broken our friendship—definitely."

"That's news to me."

"It is news to everybody, but you are not to spread it," Satchley told him. "I am doing this because I admire you and your mother. Your mother is an estimable woman, trying to get along and better herself in the world, and I know that you are both ambitious. I am afraid that you both are being victimized."

"Just—just what do you mean?" the boy asked.

"I know that Brayton has been cultivating you—and others. I know, also, that he has been selling stock in a company he formed—a corporation associated with the rubber trade."

The boy turned to face him, wild-eyed.

"Isn't—isn't that all right?" he asked.

"My poor George! If you have thrown any money into that scheme you have thrown it into the sewer," Satchley told him. "I know the scheme well. Brayton has told you that he has a substitute for rubber. He planned a big factory in South America, away up the Amazon. The stuff was to be made there, sent down the stream, and marketed as genuine rubber. He has declared that it could be produced at a fraction of a cent a pound, and that the profits would be enormous."

"It—it looked good, Mr. Satchley. So much rubber is used."

"In the first place, George, the substitute would fool nobody if it was made. And it would be a swindle at that. And the substitute cannot be manufactured except at a prohibitive price. It is a get-rich-quick scheme, George, where Brayton is the only man who gets rich quick. His directors are dummies, of course; crooked friends of his. And do you know what has happened? Brayton and his friends have unloaded their own stock. And those who have paid in money will find themselves in control, able to elect their own directors and all that—in control of a lot of worthless stock certificates and ten acres of land in South America that is not worth a dollar an acre. And you can't very well make a howl to the authorities, because the thing is a swindle on its face, and you can't go into court with clean hands. All you get for your money, my boy, are those pretty stock certificates."

"I—I can't believe it!" the boy gasped. "And yet —I've been suspicious for a week or more."

"Buck up! I was stung when I was a youngster."

"But—you can't realize what this means to me! The dirty crook! Are you sure? I want to be certain!"

"Come with me to my office, George, and I'll show you a report I received from a commercial agency. It was that report that caused me to call

Brayton a scoundrel and part with him. Our friendship is at an end. I'll give you the proof, George, but you must not say that I did so."

"I gave you my word!" the boy said.

"Very good! Come along," Satchley said.

They hurried to Satchley's office, and Satchley put the proof before him. George Gray's face grew white as he read and listened. He staggered like an intoxicated man when he got out of the chair and started toward the door.

"You must not say that I told you," Satchley warned him. "And you must do nothing foolish, my boy. Let it be a lesson to you."

"But you—you don't know all it means to me," the boy said, on the verge of tears.

"It wouldn't do any good to go into court, George. I know his methods, and you may be sure that he has protected himself, has done everything in a legal manner. And the thing was really a swindle, you know."

"I'll not go into court, Mr. Satchley!"

"Nothing foolish, now!"

"I know what I'll do. And thanks, Mr. Satchley, for putting me wise to all this."

He grasped his hat and dashed out the door, slamming it after him like an angry man. Peter Satchley leaned back in his desk chair, struck a match and lighted a cigar, and blew a cloud of smoke toward the ceiling.

"So!" he said. "We have started things, Mr. Brayton! Swindle me, will you? You'll wish you hadn't, before I'm done!"

CHAPTER VIII

THAT afternoon about four o'clock, George Brown, haberdasher, opened the door of Madame Violette's beauty parlor and crept inside like a fugitive from justice, or a runaway son returning to the home fireside and uncertain of his welcome.

Madame Violette happened to be in the front room, and she walked toward Brown swiftly, her face alight. She knew that Brown ran the shop on the first floor, for she had stopped in there several times with Raoul when he bought cravats, and once to make sundry purchases for herself, to be given as Christmas presents.

"This is a pleasure, Mr. Brown," she said. "I think you never have visited my establishment before."

"Well, I don't drop into beauty parlors very often," George Brown admitted. "It seems sissy to me for a man to have his nails trimmed every few days, and polished like his shoes."

Brown attempted a grin, and Madame Violette smiled in reply.

"This is a special occasion," Brown continued, "and, having decided that I'd get a manicure, I thought I'd come here. You trade with me, and so does your son, and I like to return favor for favor."

"Thank you," Madame Violette said.

"I aim to get a manicure. To-night the Haber-dashers' Association is giving its annual ball, and I'm on the floor committee. It's the one night in the year when I shine."

The haberdasher smiled as one pleased. Madame Violette motioned for him to follow her toward the table in the corner.

"This is Miss Margaret Dranger, Mr. Brown," she said. "She will give you a manicure. I hope to see you in my establishment often hereafter."

Madame Violette hastened away, and George Brown sat down across the table from Margaret and extended one of his hands.

"I don't know much about this kind of business, so you'll have to give orders," he said. "I generally manicure my own nails. Warm, isn't it?"

"Very," Margaret admitted.

"I don't remember seeing you come down the stairs much. Most of Madame Violette's girls walk down the stairs, and I can see them from my shop."

"I only came to work yesterday," Margaret said.

"Oh! Belong in town?"

"I came from Chicago."

"That's tough!" Brown said sympathetically. "Hope you'll like it here. You'll be lonesome at first, I suppose. There's a lot of people in New York, but it's the greatest place in the world for a person to be lonesome."

He appraised her well as she bent over his hand, and he felt his heart begin to hammer at his ribs.

George Brown had been so busy since boyhood building up a little business that he had had no time for girls. In the dim and distant future there were a wife and family, of course, but Brown had felt that they were very dim and distant.

"I've an idea," he said presently.

"Yes?"

"The haberdashers' annual ball to-night is at the hall down the street a couple of blocks. It'll be a good dance—dandy music and everything, and supper. I'm on the floor committee, you know. Why don't you let me take you to the dance?"

Margaret looked up at him, gently startled.

"You must be lonesome," he rushed on, "and I hate to see anybody lonesome. I remember how lonesome I used to be when I first came to the city. Say that you'll come. Madame Violette knows me; knows that I'm all right. I'll see that you have plenty of partners, too—nice men in my line of business."

"Thank you," said Margaret, "but——"

"Oh, I know that we've just met, and all that, but you want to forget it. I haven't any girl, you see. I'm too busy to get acquainted with girls. I've been working night and day building up my business. It'll be wonderful if you'll let me take you. All the other chaps will open their eyes to see Brown come in with a girl—especially such a pretty one."

"I'm afraid you're inclined to be a flatterer," Margaret told him.

"Nothing of the sort! I'm just speaking the truth!" Brown declared. "Where do you live?"

"I board with Mrs. Murphy."

"Better and better! I used to board there myself. Half the men and women in this part of town have boarded with Mrs. Murphy at some time or other. You ask her about George Brown—she'll tell you that I'm all right. I'd certainly like to take you to that dance. Better let me call for you."

"Very well," Margaret said. "I'll go."

And so began an acquaintance that led to great things.

George Brown, his manicure finished, paid his check as Madame Violette came back into the room.

"I've asked Miss Dranger to go to the dance with me, and she has consented," he reported. "I told her that you'd say I was all right. How about it?"

"I'm quite sure that Miss Dranger couldn't go to the dance with a better man," Madame Violette said.

"See there?" Brown asked Margaret. "I'll call for you about eight thirty—have to get there early because I'm on the floor committee."

He bowed to them, whirled around, and started to open the door. But it was opened suddenly from the outside, and Brown collided with Lorenzo Brayton as he entered.

"Pardon!" Brown exclaimed.

"You seem to be in a rush, Brown," Brayton said.

"Haberdashers' ball to-night," Brown explained. "Been getting a manicure."

"I thought you were a sober business man, Brown. A financier should not be flighty and indulge in balls and manicures."

"What did you come here for?"

"I confess I came for a manicure," Brayton said, laughing. "Maybe I'll drop in at the dance to-night."

"Wear your *rubbers*—it may rain," Brown told him. He laughed lightly and winked at Lorenzo Brayton, and Brayton winked in return.

George Brown walked the length of the corridor to the head of the stairs and started down the flight to his own establishment on the first floor. But he stopped suddenly at the spectacle of Madame Violette's son ascending.

"Great thunder!" Brown ejaculated; it was his favorite strong expression.

His first opinion, which was verified quickly, was that the boy had had access to somebody's private stock of liquor, and that what he had drunk had gone to his head. But the liquor was not all. There was a wild light in the boy's eyes, a dangerous gleam.

"What's the trouble with you?" Brown demanded. "Been looking upon the wine, little Raoul?"

"My name is George, the same as yours, and the last name is Gray," came the reply.

"All right, Gray. Why the big party?"

"There'll be a party, all right!"

"What seems to be troubling you?" Brown demanded. "You're in no condition, young man, to go parading through the front room of your mother's beauty parlor when customers are there.   Want to ruin her business?"

George Gray laughed raucously.   "A little more ruin won't hurt now," he said.

"Let me slip you a word of advice.   You go around and enter the rear way, young man.   And the next time some friend sets out a bottle of the stuff that they used to sell over bars, you turn your back and do a Marathon in the opposite direction.   Red liquor isn't any tipple for a babe like you."

"I'm a babe, all right!" said Madame Violette's son.   "I'm a sucker, a come-on!   I'm an easy mark! But maybe I'm not done yet!"

"If there is something on your mind, get it off," Brown commanded.

"That's all—I'm a babe!"

"I thought you were a seasoned business man as wise as they are found."

"Rub it in," George Gray said.

"I don't know what you're talking about, little one, and I can't even guess.   But I do know that you're drunk and angry—and that's a bad combination."

"It'll be a bad combination for one man, all right!   When I see Brayton——"

"Brayton?" said Brown, in some surprise.

"Maybe he's stung you, too," George Gray said, lurching forward, clinging to Brown's arm, his breath coming in gasps.   "Maybe you're another easy mark.   If you've dabbled in that rubber thing of his——"

"See here, what are you talking about? I'm interested," Brown said.

"Interested, are you? If you were in my boots, you'd be interested. The crook! I'll—I'll kill him!"

"S-s-sh!" Brown warned.

"I don't care who hears me. A friend gave me a tip—and showed me the proof. It's a nice little swindling game! His stock isn't worth the paper it's printed on! And I was to be rich— rich!"

The boy was almost sobbing now. George Brown's face suddenly had gone white. He grasped Madame Violette's son by the arm and started him back down the stairs.

"We'll go into my private office," Brown explained. "I want you to tell me more about this."

Being intoxicated, and having been wronged, George Gray was more than willing to talk. He explained at length, making a rambling statement, from which Brown picked out the facts, telling Brown that he had seen the report of the commercial agency and what it said. He related what Peter Satchley had told him, but he remembered his word of honor and would not tell the haberdasher from whom he had obtained the information.

This one thing kept a little hope in Brown's breast, though he told himself that it was useless to hope, and that the statement of Madame Violette's son was more than the fancy of an intoxicated man. Presently he sent the boy up the stairs again, with the advice to enter his mother's apartment by the rear door, and then went back into his office and sat down before the desk.

Brown decided that he would wait and make sure of the facts before saying or doing anything. For, if he was hit, he was hit hard. He had trusted Lorenzo Brayton, almost against his own good business judgment.

· Now ruin stared him in the face if George Gray's story was a true one. He saw the work of years melting away—his hard-earned and harder-saved dollars going to enrich the purse of a common swindler.

He realized, too, that he would have no recourse in law. Brayton was a clever man; undoubtedly he had played the game in a way to escape legal consequences. He was surprised that he did not want to go to Brayton's office and shoot him down. But anger was to come later, when he was sure— just now he felt nothing but sorrow.

"And to-night is the dance—and I'm going to take a girl!" he muttered.

CHAPTER IX

TURNING back into the beauty parlor after Brown had closed the door, Lorenzo Brayton found Madame Violette standing before him, her face flushed and her manner mildly enthusiastic. Now that she was in Brayton's presence again, she felt sure that Madame Moonshine had lied, and that all would be well.

"I had expected to see you yesterday afternoon, my dear Mr. Brayton," Madame Violette said.

"And I fully intended to pay a visit to your establishment, but the heat made me ill, and I left my office and went home early," Brayton told her. "I was alone in my office—and fainted. Frand found me on the floor."

Madame Violette expressed her sympathy instantly, which was exactly what Brayton thought she would do. He had learned years before that, in dealing with a woman, it always is well to arouse her sympathy, to appeal to the mother instinct.

"But I am feeling fine to-day," he continued. "It was just the heat—and a touch of indigestion. When a man has to eat in restaurants and hotels continually——"

He waved a hand to express his inability to explain the matter, and he knew that he had touched another tender spot in the heart of Madame Violette. Every woman thinks herself most capable of attending to the wants of the man she prefers.

"And you want your manicure?" she asked.

"Yes."

"Here is a new girl to attend you—Margaret Dranger. I am sure that you'll like her, Mr. Brayton, for she is very skillful. Be careful of his tender left thumb, Margaret, my dear. And— er—by the way, Mr. Brayton, after you have finished I'll manage to have those business papers ready, if you care to step into my parlor for them."

Madame Violette, as did Madame Moonshine, thought that this was subterfuge. But none of her girls was around to hear except Margaret, and she did not seem to be paying any attention. Brayton sat down at Margaret's table, and Madame Violette went into her parlor.

Margaret Dranger's head was bent as she began work, and Brayton was unable to see that her face was flushed and that she was fighting to regain her composure, which she had lost at his entrance. Her hands trembled a bit at first, too, but soon she was herself again and went on with her work.

"So you are a new girl," Brayton said.

"Yes; I came from Chicago." She raised her head as she spoke, and looked him straight in the eyes for a moment. Brayton decided instantly that she had lovely eyes.

"Chicago, eh?" he said. "Great town!"

"Have you ever been in Chicago?" she asked, glancing up at him again.

"Rather. I was in business there a few years ago, before I came to New York. Great place for business—Chicago! I suppose you did manicuring there?"

"At times. I am also a stenographer," Margaret replied. "So you see I generally can get a job of some sort. My last work as stenographer was with the Bethwell Printing Company."

She raised her head once more and endeavored to look him straight in the eyes, but Lorenzo Brayton happened to be glancing across the room.

"Er—lose your job there?" he asked.

"Yes. The firm failed. Mr. Bethwell, who owned the greater share, had been speculating heavily, and his investments proved to be worthless. He didn't save anything at all, I understand. One of his competitors bought the machinery and stock, and as he had his own office force there was no place for me."

"That was hard luck," Brayton commented. "And so you have taken to manicuring again. I should think that you'd greatly prefer office work. I may need another stenographer myself soon, and I'm sure I'd be glad——"

"Thank you," she interrupted, "but I am of the opinion that I shall stick to the beauty parlor for a time—unless I have hard luck here, too."

"Hard luck here?"

"I mean, unless Madame Violette speculates unwisely and becomes bankrupt, or something like that. I certainly hope not, for this seems a pleasant place to work."

"Madame Violette's speculations are small," Brayton told her. "I know, because I handle them."

"I didn't suppose that a man like you would bother with small amounts," said Margaret.

"Only now and then, to please ladies I like," Brayton replied. "I am always glad to be of assistance, when it does not make too great a demand upon my time."

"I understand."

"If you wish to make a lucrative investment at any time command me," Brayton told her.

"Thank you again, Mr. Brayton, but since I saw what happened to Mr. Bethwell, I am a little afraid of investments. They wrecked his life."

"No doubt—no doubt! He lost heavily, you say?"

"He was swindled!" Margaret Dranger said. "He believed in a man and trusted him with almost all his funds. It was the knowledge that this man was a scoundrel that hurt Mr. Bethwell as much as the loss of his money. Now Mr. Bethwell is in a—a sanitarium. His nerves are shattered and——"

"Dear me!"

"And, of course, the guilty man disappeared," Margaret went on to say. "Somebody should find the scoundrel and punish him. But I suppose that he has changed his name long before this. He called himself Tampley there."

Again her eyes met those of Lorenzo Brayton, but there was no unusual expression in his save a slight flicker that might have been caused by nervousness. Margaret Dranger bent over his hand and continued her work.

"There are a lot of swindlers in the country," Brayton said. "People should be very careful to whom they intrust their money."

"I agree with you."

The manicure was finished. Margaret sat back from the table and began preparing the check for the cashier.

"By the way," she said. "I think that I know of somebody who does want to invest."

"Indeed?"

"Yes. A gentleman was in here yesterday afternoon speaking about it, and he mentioned you and wanted to know whether you were a good broker. I had to tell him, of course, that I was a newcomer and did not know you, but Madame Violette told him that you were an excellent business man."

"I shall have to thank her."

"The gentleman said that he was a manufacturer's agent, and that his name was Rathway."

He paid the amount of his check, and then walked across to the door of Madame Violette's private parlor and tapped upon it lightly with his knuckles. A cheery voice bade him enter, and Lorenzo Brayton did so, his hat in his hand, a smile upon his face.

The door closed. Margaret Dranger stood looking at it for some time, deep in thought.

"Come out of the trance!" the cashier called.

"I—I detest him!" Margaret said tensely.

"I'm with you there," the cashier declared. "I don't like the look in his eyes. If I handed him any of my money to invest I'd certainly kiss it good-by!

Watch the shop, will you, while I run back and speak to one of the other girls?"

Margaret nodded that she would, and the cashier hurried away. Still standing beside her table, Margaret Dranger continued to look at the door through which Lorenzo Brayton had gone. In her face was deadly hatred, in her eyes the light that blasts.

CHAPTER X

MADAME VIOLETTE was waiting in the middle of the room. She turned with a smile upon her face as Lorenzo Brayton entered. The velvet curtain before the dais was thrown back, and Brayton could see the crystal globe in its frame.

"It seems an age since I saw you last," Madame Violette said.

Brayton put his hat down and advanced toward her. They were like two antagonists measuring each other. On her part, Madame Violette had determined to ascertain whether Madame Moonshine had spoken the truth, whether Brayton was a double-dealing scoundrel or an honest man worthy of a woman's love.

Brayton, for his part, realized that the atmosphere was charged with danger. His illegal dealings had made him quick to read the human mind. He sensed, without knowing how he did it, that Madame Violette, for the first time since he had met her, was doubting him; and Brayton felt called upon to remove the doubt, since it was a menace.

So each was on guard, determined to play a game of wits. Madame Violette wanted to lull Brayton into a feeling of security and then try to catch him in a trap—if he was guilty. Brayton, on the other hand, wanted to make this woman more infatuated than before. There was no doubt of him mirrored in her face, but Brayton knew that doubt was in her mind.

"So you miss me if you do not see me every day?" he asked.

"To be sure I do!"

"And I miss you, Violette!" he declared. "But a busy man must attend to business, you know. You don't know how I appreciate these little visits with you. They are restful."

"And yet I am afraid that they must stop," she said.

"Why is that?"

"Lorenzo, I am afraid that people are commencing to talk, and a woman in my position cannot endure that, of course. I have to be very careful. I run a beauty parlor, and I have a number of young girls working for me."

"People talking?" he gasped.

"Our little conferences have been noticed, and I fear that some think they are not all business. I—I have had a distressing scene with Madame Moonshine."

"The modiste?"

"Yes. She dropped in to see me, and we talked of you. Lorenzo, that woman must have been spying upon us!"

Brayton scarcely could hold back a smile. Her words were almost identical with those of Madame Moonshine. Well, he had persuaded Madame Moonshine, and so he should be able to persuade Madame Violette in the same manner.

"Tell me about it," he said.

"She—she spoke of sly kisses given along with tips regarding investments. Just think of it, Lorenzo! That woman! And then she had the audacity to tell me that she was the recipient of your kisses, too, and that you were giving her a chance to invest, and—and intended to marry her!"

"My dear Violette! You are a woman old enough to have common sense, and that is one reason I have been attracted to you. Do you not know how a jealous woman works?"

"I—I thought of that—that she was deceiving me."

"What else?" Brayton asked. "I may as well tell you—though the subject is distasteful—that Madame Moonshine has—shall I say—made advances to me? In truth, she has deliberately thrown herself at me. What can a man do in such a case?"

"The creature!"

"Her intentions were honest enough, I suppose. She hoped possibly to interest me so that I would propose marriage. Could I do that—when I know you?"

"Oh, Lorenzo!"

"This brings matters to a crisis, my dear Violette! I had hoped to wait until my big business deal had been consummated. But I ask you now to be my wife. Surely you have seen the state of my feelings toward you."

Madame Violette blushed and hung her head.

"You are sure?" she asked.

"I am sure, Violette, else I would not have spoken."

"You make me very happy, Lorenzo. I shall try to make you a dutiful wife."

She surrendered her lips to his kiss, and then sat down again, moving her chair a bit closer.

"One thing I must ask you, Lorenzo," Madame Violette said. "I know that you are rich now, and soon will be very wealthy—and that even my poor investment will bring in large returns. But there is my boy, my baby. He wants to make his own way in the world, and you have said that he is a born financier. Promise me, Lorenzo, that after we are married you'll give him a little attention, set him on the right track."

"I shall take a pride in doing it," Brayton replied. It pleased Brayton to think of himself setting another man on the right track. Had Madame Violette wanted him to instruct her son in the principles of crookdom—if crookdom has principles—it would have been more to the point.

"And when——" Madame Violette scarcely could voice the question that was in her heart.

"It will be difficult, especially for me, but I think we had best keep our happiness a secret for a short time longer," Brayton said. "I want to conclude this big deal, and then I need think of nothing but love."

"Oh, Lorenzo!"

"A man should not mix business and affection."

"And the business is all right?" she asked. She had been worrying a bit about that.

"Everything is lovely," Brayton replied. "I expect to sell a half interest to a big corporation for many times what we have invested, and still retain valuable stock. You can have everything your heart desires, my dear."

Madame Violette looked as though she expected another kiss, and Brayton obliged her. His conscience had been dead for some years, and hence did not bother him. He drew her toward him.

"Do not forget," he added, "that just now we must tell no one."

"I shall not forget, Lorenzo. But I hate to keep the happy secret. I am bubbling over with joy."

"It will be but for a short time," he said. "I must give all my attention to the big deal. We do not want anything unfortunate to happen now, beloved."

"I understand, Lorenzo. And we'll be married as soon as the big deal is completed?"

"The very next day," Brayton declared.

"And that foolish Madame Moonshine! You are sure, Lorenzo, that she means nothing to you?"

"Madame Moonshine? She means less than nothing to me!" Brayton said, for he knew that was what Madame Violette wanted to hear.

The door from the beauty parlor opened. Madame Moonshine, her face livid, stepped into the room. Brayton did not doubt that she, too, had heard.

CHAPTER XI

MURDER MAD

MADAME VIOLETTE bridled instantly, and then her woman's intuition seemed to tell her that something was radically wrong, and that this was more than a simple intrusion. For Madame Moonshine was not looking at her, but at Lorenzo Brayton, and her face was that of a woman scorned.

Brayton could do nothing except stand at the foot of the dais, his face incrutable, and wonder what was to happen. His mind was working swiftly, but for once it seemed to fail him in an emergency. So he waited, groping meanwhile for a way out of his difficulty.

"So Madame Moonshine means nothing to you?" she cried. "And you are to marry Violette as soon as the big deal is completed, are you? Scoundrel!"

"Madame!" Violette exclaimed. "Have the kindness to remember that you are standing in my house, and that you are speaking of my future husband."

"You'll not want him for a husband when I am through," Madame Moonshine declared. "You did not believe me yesterday, but perhaps you will believe me now. And I did not believe you! Had I done so, it would have saved me two hundred dollars, at least."

Brayton seemed to come out of a trance. "If you

ladies are going to indulge in a dispute, perhaps I
had better retire," he said, bowing to them.

"You'll remain where you are until this matter is
settled!" Madame Moonshine cried. "Monster!
Wretch! Brute!"

"What is this? What is it?" Violette cried. "Are
you insane, woman?"

"If I am not, it is not the fault of Lorenzo Brayton. So he would make you his bride, would he, as
soon as the big deal is completed? He promised me
the same thing, Madame Violette, within an hour
after luncheon to-day."

"I'll not believe it!"

"Look at the man! Oo, la, la! Look at his face
and then say that you do not believe."

For Brayton had been unable to control his
countenance, and for once he betrayed his guilt. Before men he had swindled no doubt he would have
remained calm, but before him now were two women
with whose affections he had trifled, and Brayton
feared women.

"I suspected the wretch despite his honeyed words,
and I watched him," Madame Moonshine continued.
"I waited until he came in here, and then I entered
the beauty parlor, sent the girl for a jar of cold
cream, and listened at the door. Yes, I, Madame
Moonshine, listened at the door—even as you, Violette accused me of doing yesterday. What fools
women are!"

"I—I cannot believe it," Madame Violette said
again.

"He asked me to be his wife and declared that he

had no feeling at all for you. And then he came to you and said that he wanted to marry you, and declared that Moonshine was less than nothing to him. The wretch!"

"But why—why?"

"He has been playing his little game. Thank the good Heaven that my eyes are open at last! I was to be rich, and help him spend his wealth. We were to travel, spend our hours in doing nothing but being happy! And he told you the same thing. Violette, did he not?"

"But why?"

"Because he has made love to us, and then got our money."

"Our money?"

"For his precious rubbber company!" Madame Moonshine went on. "We think we love him, are going to marry him, and we invest! Oo, la, la! For Moonshine to be caught in such an old trap! We are but weak, foolish women."

"But the investment is all right!" Madame Violette declared, though she was commencing to think differently.

"Is it? Or is it as valueless as his pretended love?" Madame Moonshine cried.

Lorenzo Brayton cleared his throat and held up a hand for silence. They granted it, eager for his explanation.

"Perhaps," Brayton said, "I have done some things that were a little irregular. Not every man could choose between two such charming ladies."

"The time for pretty speeches is past!" Madame Moonshine interrupted.

"Explain!" Violette cried.

"I—I scarcely can explain," Brayton declared. "When I was in the company of Madame Moonshine, I felt sure that I wanted her for my wife. And when I was visiting Madame Violette, I felt that she was the woman I loved. A too abundant affection always has been my curse. I was in a quandary. Perhaps I would have asked neither of you until I was sure, but each of you said that there had been some talk, and as a gentleman I could do nothing less than offer my hand, could I?"

"Wretch!" Madame Moonshine cried again.

"And what—what are you going to do now?" Violette asked, tears in her voice.

"Yes, what are you going to do?" Madame Moonshine echoed. "Do you think that it is a light thing to trifle with the heart of Moonshine? Do you think that you shall go unpunished? You have made a laughingstock of me! My own saleswomen and models will chuckle behind my back! Have I lived for this? I could kill you!"

"Speak, Lorenzo!" Violette commanded.

"What can I say?" Brayton asked. "Suppose I take my leave, and we will all consider the affair."

"You'll remain here for the present," Madame Moonshine declared. "There is another matter. I can see why you did it—so that two foolish women would hand you their money. Only to-day, after promising to marry me, you got two hundred dollars more—for your precious rubber corporation. You told me that you were letting me have the stock as a favor, despite the fact that great financiers were struggling to get it."

"You told me that, too, Lorenzo!" Violette interrupted.

"It is a pretty game he has been playing. I have stripped my business to buy stock, because I thought that he was in love with me. The savings of years——"

"And mine!" Madame Violette cried. "The savings of years, of which my son did not know! I was afraid that Raoul would not approve. Tell me, Lorenzo—the money is safe, is it not? Even if you are fickle in your love, the money is safe—the savings of years!"

"Rest assured of that," Brayton said, trying to be calm. "Both of you ladies have invested funds in an enterprise that is sure to succeed. Have no fears regarding the financial end of this affair. I regret that my love-making has caused so much misery. I have tried to explain. I cannot marry both of you, of course."

"And how do we know that the money is safe?" Madame Moonshine demanded. "How do we know that you did not make love to us so that you could swindle us?"

"I assure you——" Brayton began.

The door leading to the rear room of Madame Violette's apartment was thrown open violently. They whirled around to find Violette's son standing there. His face was flushed, his hair unkempt. Anger blazed in his eyes.

"You—crook!" he shouted at Lorenzo Brayton.

"My dear Raoul, what do you mean?" Brayton stammered.

"You know what I mean. So you've been stealing from women, too, have you? I was in there—I heard! You've made love to my foolish mother, and robbed her! You've done the same with Madame Moonshine! You've robbed George Brown, too, and Heaven knows how many more. And you've stolen from me."

"Raoul, what are you saying?" Madame Violette asked.

"Don't call me Raoul—my name is George Gray. What am I saying? That this crook came to me and praised me, told me what a great business man I was! He flattered me. He found out my ambition, and said he'd help me. Do you know how he helped? By getting me to buy stock in that rubbber company. He coaxed me until I gave him all the money for pretty stock certificates. Mother, we haven't any bank account except enough to meet current expenses. We're wiped out! I used the money to buy stock."

"My boy! My boy!" Madame Violette cried.

He was a boy in truth now. He crept to his mother's arms for comfort and wept there, unashamed. But soon he held up his head again.

"All gone!" he said. "We have to begin again. That's the kind of financier I am. I trusted that crook to——"

"Don't be hasty, my son, because of what you have overheard. Perhaps you did invest too much, but if the company is all right——"

Her son thrust her away. "All right!" he said with a sneer. "It isn't all right. I haven't thought so for some time, and now I have the proof. The money's lost, I tell you. He's nothing but a cheap swindler."

"My boy!"

"It's the truth. Look at him! He steals from women and boys, from men with but a few dollars in the world!"

"But the company——" Madame Violette began.

"Some of his crooked friends are dummy directors. The company is no good. I've seen the report of a commercial agency. It's crooked on the face of it. Can't you see? We were to manufacture a substitute for rubber and sell it for the real thing, at a big profit. It can't be manufactured as cheap as he said. It's a fake! And do you know what else he's done?"

"Wait, Raoul! Wait, George! Mr. Brayton's money is in it, too. Can't you understand that?"

"Certainly!" Brayton said, thinking that he saw the way out. "My boy, some enemy of mine has been telling you these things."

"Don't lie to me!" cried Madame Violette's son. "I'll tell you what you did. You formed your fake company, and kept all the stock except a few shares. It's your stock that you've been selling, not treasury stock. You've unloaded almost all of it. You're out of the company. We, who have bought from you, own a lot of worthless certificates, while you've got the money—par value! You crook!"

"Mr. Brayton, is this true?" Violette demanded.

"Of course it is true!" her son declared. "Look at

his face; you can read the truth there! He's ruined us—played with us—robbed us! All the money we had saved——"

"All I had saved!" Madame Moonshine interrupted.

"And now we've got him!" Raoul cried. "We've got him, and I'm going to end him!"

He lurched forward as he spoke, and pulled a revolver from his pocket!

CHAPTER XII

THE VICTIMS

RAOUL! Raoul!"

Madame Violette's cry expressed misery, fright, warning. Madame Moonshine was cringing against the wall in sudden fear. Lorenzo Brayton's face went white and his lower jaw sagged, and it seemed as though he would collapse utterly because of the menace of the weapon the boy held, its muzzle toward him, and because of the look of murder in the boy's face.

"My boy!"

Madame Violette was thoroughly alive to the situation in an instant. In a flash she saw the crime, an arrest, a long and expensive trial and the misery of waiting for the verdict. She hurled herself upon her son, upon the weapon he held, so that he could not fire for fear of wounding her. The tension snapped, for the boy could not maintain it for long. A great sob came from him, and he dropped the revolver to the floor. He was but a child again for the time being.

"Go—go!" Madame Violette shouted at Brayton, looking around at him. "We'll deal with you later."

"Yes, go, you crook!" Madame Moonshine shrieked, holding the door open. "Go, robber!"

Lorenzo Brayton picked up his hat and passed into

the front room of the beauty parlor, his face still ashen, his form trembling, for he had looked Death in the face and knew it, and through his mind had flashed what Detective Sam Haynes of the homicide squad had said—that some detectives are able to feel a crime coming—and he remembered, too, that Haynes had been hanging around the building, for no apparent reason.

Behind him he left two hopeless women and a youth who had lost faith in men and life. Raoul sobbed for a time against his mother's breast, and then sat down near the window.

"My poor boy!" she said. "You cannot have your office now, not for years and years. I bought stock with all my money."

"And I used all except enough for current bills." The boy moaned. "We'll have to start building up again."

"And he stripped me clean!" Madame Moonshine declared. There was a hard look in her face as she spoke.

"Perhaps it is not so bad." Madame Violette expressed her faint hope.

But her son cut her short. "No use talking like that," he said. "The money is gone. Oh, he's been legal enough, all right. He can sit back and grin, and what are we going to do about it?"

"There are many things that can be done," Madame Moonshine said, her voice ominous.

"Not for a woman to do!" Raoul exclaimed. "Why didn't you let me kill him when I had the chance? Well, there'll be other chances."

"Don't talk that way, my baby!" Madame Violette cried. "You must do nothing! They'd arrest you, maybe put you in prison, maybe send you to the electric chair!"

"I'd be willing to go to the chair to get even with him!"

"Hush! Leave that for others," his mother told him. "We are suffering enough as it is. You are young; you must not mar your life. Others—who are older——"

"Not you! Not you!" the boy cried.

Madame Moonshine crossed the room to the window and stood for a time looking down at the street. Presently she turned toward the others.

"We have been foolish women, Violette," she said. "I ask you to forgive me. See what a man can do to break friendship between women!"

For a moment she was clasped in Madame Violette's arms, and then they dried their tears.

As for Lorenzo Brayton, he had recovered his composure before he had reached the ground floor. He hurried through the lobbby and ascended to his office, and went into the inner room and closed the door.

Brayton had endured such scenes many times in his career, but generally with men only. The culmination of each swindling game was such a scene, but Brayton took it all as a part of the business and thought of the profits with some degree of comfort.

"It'll blow over in a week," he told himself.

What puzzled him was how the truth had become public so soon. He had expected a week longer in

which to unload the last few hundred dollars' worth
of stock. But, as it was, the profits were enormous
and he could afford to undergo some slight annoyance.

The boy, he supposed, had grown suspicious and
had gone to some reputable financier for advice, and
the report from the commercial agency had followed.
Then he remembered that Satchley had had a report
from a commercial agency!

"Satchley!" he gasped. "Pete Satchley did it!
The crook—trying to get square that way! Well,
I've made my pile out of it. Satchley hasn't done
me much harm at that, and maybe he'll be satisfied
now."

But Peter Satchley was not satisfied. He had
watched Madame Violette's son carefully, and then
had dropped a hint here and there that had caused
the story to travel like a fire before a raging wind.
Peter Satchley knew a number of persons who had
invested in Brayton's fake rubber company, and he
made certain that the truth had reached all of them.

Brayton spent the remainder of the afternoon in
his office doing routine work, and at the usual time
left the office and went to the elevator. His manner
was nothing out of the ordinary as he nodded to
several acquaintances. On the ground floor he
stopped to purchase some cigars, intending to get a
taxicab and hurry home, eat dinner and spend the
evening reading. Experience had taught him that,
after a crash, it was best to live quietly for a few
days and pretend an innocence that did not exist.

He filled his cigar case, lighted one of the weeds—

and turned around to find himself confronted by Brown, the haberdasher. Brayton sensed instantly that Brown knew the true state of affairs, and he did not like the expression in the haberdasher's face. He opened his mouth to speak, but Brown was before him.

"So it was a fake!" Brown said, in a low tone.

"I—I beg your pardon?" Brayton gasped.

"Don't try to act in front of me. It was a fake—a swindle! So you have nicked the easy marks, have you, and I am one of them? You've got a smooth tongue, all right, Brayton. I actually thought you were an honest man."

"Brown——" began Brayton.

"Don't lie any more!" Brown warned him. "Serves me right, I suppose, for dabbling in stocks. Well, you plucked me nicely, Brayton! You got all my savings, all the money I had intended to use in enlarging my business. I've been working hard for ten years—and I find that I have been working for you!"

"Somebody betrayed our plans——" Brayton began.

"Don't lie! I'm wise, Brayton. I can't touch you legally, I suppose, but I can touch you physically!"

Brown's tone changed and he launched himself forward. Brayton had been looking for it, and he darted nimbly to one side. But he was not to escape so easily. Haberdasher Brown had been allowing his anger to gather, and he was determined to mark his man.

A woman screamed; half a score of men started

forward along the lobbby to stop the fight. Brayton darted to a corner by the elevator cage and prepared to defend himself.

Brown did not strike him as he stood there. Brown reached under Brayton's guard, caught him by the collar of the coat, and jerked him into the open.

"Fight, you crook!" he cried, and his open palm rang against Brayton's cheek.

Brayton, furious at the indignity, swung wildly at his antagonist. He dodged Brown's next blow. And then a third man hurled himself into the battle. It was Detective Sam Haynes.

"Stop it!" he commanded. "What's this row about? Want me to pinch both of you?"

"That—cursed—crook!" Brown cried out.

"I'll make you prove that!" Brayton exclaimed. "I'll have you up for slander. You heard him, Haynes!"

"Yes, and he can hear me again, and everybody else around here can hear me. You're a crook, you're a grafter and a swindler! And if you haul me into court, I'll prove it!"

"Be quiet!" Detective Haynes told him. "What's the trouble, Brayton?"

"I invested a few hundred dollars for this man, at his own direction," Brayton replied. "The investment has proved a failure, and now he wants to take it out on me. He's a piker!"

"And you're a swindler!" Brown shouted.

"Shut up!" Haynes commanded again. "Want to prefer a charge against him, Brayton?"

"No; it isn't serious enough for that. But I want him warned not to annoy me again."

"Fair enough," Haynes said. "You understand that, Brown? If you have any kick coming, go to court and start a suit."

"And a lot of good it would do me!" Brown exclaimed. "He's framed the thing well, all right. All I'd get in court would be a laugh. I don't have to go to court—there are other ways."

The haberdasher gave Brayton a last look of mingled fury and hate and whirled around and entered his shop. Lorenzo Brayton, with the eyes of a score of men upon him, controlled his nervousness enough to light a fresh cigar, for he realized that this was a moment to show bravado.

"I'm obliged to you, Haynes," he said. "Several persons around this building purchased stock in a certain company through me. The idea has got about that the stock is worthless, and they are likely to blame me for it. I had stock in the same company, but sold it some time ago. Is it my fault if the others didn't have sense enough to do the same? Have a cigar, Haynes."

"No, thanks—I've got a cigar!" said Haynes as he turned away toward the crowd.

Lorenzo Brayton adjusted his cravat, dusted his hat and put it on, and started on through the lobby.

At the front entrance he came face to face with Frand, the old janitor. There was a look of intense misery in Frand's countenance as he put out a trembling hand and touched Brayton's sleeve.

"I've heard all the rumors," Frand said. "It ain't

so, sir; is it? All my savings, sir, that I need for my old age——"

"I can't be bothered now, Frand!" Brayton said gruffly. "Some things have gone wrong, yes, but we don't know how badly yet. I'm doing the best I can."

"So it is true!" Frand cried. "It's true what they say—that you're a cheat, a swindler! Why did you pick me, sir? I'll be left in my old age without a penny! Oh, why didn't you leave my little money be, sir?"

"I haven't time now——" Brayton began.

"You—you!" Frand cried incoherently. "Penniless in my old age—because you lied to me, and cheated me!"

Old Frand tottered forward, his hands held as though he would grasp Brayton's throat and choke him. Tears were streaming down the old man's cheeks. Brayton thrust out an arm and held him off, and hurried into the street.

CHAPTER XIII

THE WARNING

HAVING reached his rooms, Lorenzo Brayton called a certain private detective agency on the telephone and made his requests known; and then he ordered the apartment-house clerk not to ring his telephone for anything or anybody. The Japanese servant sensed that something was wrong, but his face remained inscrutable, as is the habit with his race, and he showed no curiosity when Brayton told him that there would be two other gentlemen for dinner.

An hour later the two arrived. They were gigantic men, and any experienced crook in the world would have said instantly that they were detectives. As a matter of fact, they belonged to a private agency which managed to conduct itself so as to remain inside the law, but at which many officials looked askance.

"You are to do bodyguard work for a few days," Brayton told them. "As your boss probably has told you, I'm a financier and broker. One of my deals has gone wrong. Perfectly legal, and all that, but some persons are dissatisfied. I was attacked to-day as I was leaving my office, and I don't want anything like that to occur again."

"We're on!" one of them said.

"You'll make yourselves at home here. Dinner will be served in a few minutes. In my den are cigars, books to read, anything you wish. You'll sleep here, of course, and to-morrow you'll go to the office with me. You'll be well paid in addition to the regular wage the agency gives you."

The following morning they accompanied Brayton to his office and waited in the front room after the manner of clients awaiting an interview with an attorney. Brayton attended to his routine business, dictated replies to letters, and refused to answer any telephone calls, having his stenographer say that he was busy in a business conference. A report of a mining company claimed the attention of Brayton that afternoon, so that he almost forgot his victims for the time being.

But his victims had not forgotten him. Murder was in the air, had Lorenzo Brayton but known it. George Brown attended to his business, but without enthusiasm. He had already taken stock. The savings and profits of ten years had vanished. The chance to enlarge his business was gone. He was to have leased the store room adjoining his shop, but found that now he could not, not possessing the necessary capital.

Brown had taken Margaret Dranger to the haberdashers' ball, and had remembered that he was a host. He had managed to dance and laugh and joke as though nothing unfortunate had happened. But, as he accompanied her back to Mary Murphy's boarding house, they spoke of the swindle. Margaret had learned of it in the beauty parlor, of course—

and she had heard her employer and Madame Moonshine wailing and had watched Raoul.

"He should be punished—punished cruelly!" Margaret declared.

"He will be punished!" George Brown answered grimly.

Madame Violette's son went around like a man who had received a blow from which he never would recover. The boy's faith in himself was gone, and also his faith in humanity. He realized that he was as bad as a thief, since he had invested the money without speaking to his mother about it first. He glanced into the future and saw his mother spending the years in the beauty parlor, and himself working hard for a living. He visualized what he could have done with the money that had gone to Lorenzo Brayton. Youth does not take such things easily.

"The crook!" Raoul muttered. "I wish I had killed him! But it isn't too late yet!"

And there was Madame Violette herself. The blow had been a severe one to her pride as well as to her purse. For the first time in years she felt her age. Her savings had gone to enrich Lorenzo Brayton. She knew now what a foolish woman she had been, and how Brayton had played upon her vanity and affection. Her heart bled for her son, too, and for the self-confidence he had lost. She knew that it would be a blow from which, perhaps, his ambition never would recover. She knew that it might affect his entire life and make a failure out of a boy who might otherwise have been a success.

"It's a big debt," Madame Violette told herself, "a big debt Lorenzo Brayton must pay!"

Madame Moonshine, sitting in her private office, knowing that her models and saleswomen had learned what had occurred, gnashed her teeth while tears of rage streaked her cheeks. The blood that flowed in her veins was blood that could heat with hatred. She could not afford the financial loss. She had expected gigantic profits and marriage with a wealthy man— and she knew that, instead, she would have difficulty in meeting her bills the first of the month.

"I could kill—kill!" she cried.

Frand was alone in the world, and old age already had placed its stamp upon him. Lorenzo Brayton's silver tongue had taken from Frand the few hundred dollars which he had saved through a lifetime and which he had expected to keep him in comfort when the day came that he was too old and feeble to work.

"I ain't got anyting to live for," he said to himself bitterly. "I might as well end it—might as well end myself, and him, too!"

The will to slay Lorenzo Brayton was in many minds—in the mind of Madame Violette, of Brown, Madame Moonshine, Raoul, old Frand, and Satchley. And there were yet others.

Brayton attended to his business as though nothing had happened. The two detectives continued to act as his bodyguard.

He avoided the beauty parlor of Madame Violette now, and had no reason for entering the shop of Madame Moonshine or that of Brown. He saw Satchley now and then, and met old Frand's accusing eyes frequently, but that was all, and it did not annoy Brayton to any great extent.

"It's blown over," he told himself. "Time to arrange for another deal now."

Then Morton Rathway called at the office and sent in his card. Brayton had him ushered into the private room and bade him be seated. The broker's fingers rested on a button that would summon the two detectives if Rathway attempted violence. But Brayton did not anticipate that; he had had no dealings with the mysterious Mr. Rathway.

"I have a bit of money to invest," Rathway said. "I want to be sure that it's in good hands, of course. People are saying things about you just now, but I want to be just and——"

Brayton bent across the desk and spoke in a confidential tone.

"I suppose there are a few persons around this building who are calling me a swindler and a scoundrel. That is a thing every reputable broker has to face now and then, and it is unjust. Those people came to me to invest money. They purchased stock in an enterprise that I thought was good—not the best in the world, but good. I had stock in it myself. I saw that things were going to pieces and tried to get out from under. I suppose that I am to blame because I didn't run around and help them unload. I've got all I can do to attend to my own business, without playing nursemaid to a lot of amateur financiers."

"Your explanation sounds all right," Rathway said. "But they are saying that you coaxed them into the thing."

"My dear Mr. Rathway, you look like a sensible man," Brayton said. "Do you think a person of my standing would waste time coaxing—as you call it—such pikers? If I coaxed anybody, it would be a man of means who could invest a million."

"Coaxing the pikers has proved a profitable game before now," Rathway said. "Some of your investors are pretty sore. I'd watch out for them, if I were you."

"I shall protect myself, naturally."

"Well, I'll think it over," said Rathway. "I've got a couple of thousand—and you might keep your eyes open for something good."

"If I suggest anything it will be something good," Brayton declared. "No sensible broker, even a crook, would try to swindle a man like you."

"Thanks!" said Rathway dryly. "You've got a nice office here, Brayton."

"Very comfortable and conveniently arranged," Brayton said.

Rathway was getting out of the chair. He glanced around the room, particularly at the filing cases and the safe.

"Well, see you later," he said. "Hope you find something good for me."

Brayton grinned after Rathway had gone. "There's one born every minute," he said.

For the two days following he watched those around the building narrowly, and then let the two detectives go. He judged that he did not need a bodyguard any longer.

Then there came a morning when he dictated replies to letters, and began the perusal of mail that had been tossed aside as personal.

The second letter attracted him. It had been addressed on a typewriter, and with red ink. Brayton ripped the envelope open and took out a single sheet of paper. He glanced at it quickly and read:

The Scarlet Scourge is about to pay you a visit. Your sins cannot be allowed to go unpunished.

There was no signature—just those few words in red. Brayton read it a second time, held the sheet of paper to the light to find that it had no watermark, and then tossed it aside.

"These movie people are going the limit in advertising," he mused. "I suppose this thing is the forerunner of the 'Horrors of Hattie' or the 'Mystifications of Myrtle.' "

He went on reading his mail, but now and then his eyes strayed to that message in red print. He sat back in the chair and considered whether it was a threat. For an instant he thought that Satchley might have sent it to frighten him; and then he told himself that Peter Satchley would do nothing so childish. Satchley would strike at him undoubtedly when he had the opportunity, but not in that manner.

When Satchley struck, there would be muscle behind the blow.

"Just a movie advertisement!" Brayton told himself again.

Scarcely knowing what he did, he folded the letter and returned it to the envelope, and put it at one side of his desk. There it remained, to be found later and to assume a certain importance.

CHAPTER XIV

PECULIAR ACTIONS

SINCE the night of the dance and the discovery of Lorenzo Brayton's perfidy, George Brown had been dropping into the beauty parlor of Madame Violette regularly. It did not take a person of extraordinary cleverness to determine that the attraction for Brown was Margaret Dranger.

Something seemed to draw him to the girl when he wanted sympathy, not so much sympathy in words as that which one feels in the presence of another perfectly attuned. He tried to tell himself that he was a fool—that now, of all times, he would have to forego all thoughts of courtship and marriage, since his savings were gone and he would have to fight his way upward again. But he continued his calls.

He made friends with Raoul, and they sat together in Madame Violette's little parlor and discussed what they would do to Lorenzo Brayton were it not against the law—and each glanced at the other furtively, as though to say that it might be done, the law notwithstanding.

Upon a certain afternoon, just before the closing hour, Brown found that there was nobody in the front parlor except Margaret Dranger and the little cashier.

Brown sat down at Margaret's table and ordered a manicure, which he did not need.

"I'm feeling blue," he said.

"You shouldn't. You're young and——"

"I know all that," he interrupted. "But I worked mighty hard for the money Brayton got out of me. It takes a man's nerve out of him to have a thing like that happen."

"The same thing happened to a man for whom I worked in Chicago," Margaret said. "He is in a sanitarium now, wrecked for life."

"Men like Brayton ought to be punished!"

"Perhaps he will be," Margaret said. "But the man who punishes him should not do it in a way that will cause himself trouble. Brayton isn't worth going to jail for."

"There have been clever punishments before now," Brown told her. "Lo you suppose, after you are through here and my shop is closed, I could have you go to dinner with me?"

"That would be foolish," she said. "I pay by the week at Mrs. Murphy's, and you need to save your money just now."

"Then couldn't I come to Mrs. Murphy's and see you afterward? We might take a walk—go to the park or somewhere."

"Not to-night, please. I'm—I'm rather tired, and I think that I shall go to bed early."

"Some other night, then?"

"Yes."

"You know, I—I like you. I've never had a chance to learn much about girls, and I'm rough and not clever, I reckon. I can't make pretty speeches. But if I was to get married, I think I'd want a girl something like you. Only I'm a fool to think of such things now—a poor fool who has handed his money over to a swindler."

"Many very clever men have done that," she replied, bending her head. "And—and you just made a very pretty speech—paid me a great compliment."

"Th-thanks," he stammered.

Brown paid his check and left the place, and Margaret Dranger gave him a soft look as he departed. It warmed Brown's heart just when that heart needed warming most.

Later in the evening, just as he was preparing to close for the day, he saw her hurry through the lobby. As she passed the interior window of the shop, she dropped her purse. She had been holding it in her hand with her handkerchief.

Brown noticed that she hurried on and did not realize the loss. He hastened into the lobby and recovered the purse, and went to the entrance. But Margaret Dranger already was halfway up the block, walking swiftly.

"In a hurry about something," Brown mused. "I'll just take it up to her to-night."

It was after ten o'clock when he arrived at Mrs. Murphy's boarding house that night, but that did not stop him. Mary Murphy was the sort of woman who sits in the front doorway summer nights until almost midnight, and Brown knew it.

She was sitting on the porch as Brown approached, and greeted him warmly.

"I—I'd like to see Miss Dranger," Brown told the landlady. "I saw her drop her purse as she left the building this evening, and picked it up. I meant to get here earlier, but I've been busy."

"The dear girl must not have missed it," Mrs. Murphy said. "At least she didn't say a word about it. Perhaps she thought that she had left it at the beauty parlor."

"If I can see her——" Brown persisted.

"It is rather late," Mrs. Murphy said. "The poor, dear girl seemed to be very tired, and I am sure that she has retired. I spoke to her less than five minutes ago; she was standing in the doorway of her room —ready for bed. I can give her the purse."

"Thanks," Brown said.

He handed the purse to Mrs. Murphy and went down the steps.

Down the street he walked slowly, intending to go home and try to get some sleep. He stopped on a corner and lighted his cigar again, and for a time stood there watching the traffic. A surface car stopped on the opposite side of the street. A girl got off it and hurried away. She was Margaret Dranger!

Brown gasped, rubbed his eyes, looked at her again. He knew that he was not mistaken. There was Margaret Dranger, who had just stepped off a car from uptown, and she was hurrying toward the boarding house.

Mary Murphy had declared to him that she had seen the girl five minutes before his visit, had seen her in the doorway of her room, prepared for retiring for the night. Mrs. Mary Murphy apparently had lied—and to anybody who knew the landlady well that was as much as saying that the world had come to an end.

Brown followed on the opposite side of the street, scarcely realizing what he was doing. The thing puzzled him. Margaret had told him that she was tired and was going to bed early; Mrs. Murphy had told him she was in her room, and probably asleep. And here she was fully dressed and on the street, evidently returning from a journey to another part of the city.

"Funny!" Brown commented, scratching his left ear, as he always did when puzzled.

He became aware then that another man was watching Margaret Dranger closely, following her, in fact. George Brown felt his head growing hot.

Brown crossed the street and walked faster. The man was ahead of him, and Margaret was ahead of the man. Then Brown saw that the man was shadowing the girl as a detective might have done. They passed beneath a bright light at the corner. The man was Morton Rathway.

He knew little of Rathway, except that he had been in the shop a few times and asked a multitude of questions about different things. He had considered Rathway more or less of a pest—had looked upon him as a newcomer trying to become acquainted with everybody in a day. And he certainly did not like his actions now.

Brown watched. Margaret came to the boarding house and darted up the steps and through the door.

Mrs. Murphy, it appeared, had already gone inside. Rathway walked past the house slowly, and Brown recrossed the street to watch him.

Rathway turned back when he reached the next corner, crossed the street himself, and stood in a dark doorway. Brown knew now that he was watching the house. In a front room on the second story a light appeared, and for an instant Brown saw a vision of Margaret Dranger as she stood before the window drawing down the shade. Still Rathway remained in the dark doorway, and Brown watched him.

Ten minutes passed; in Margaret's room the light was extinguished. Morton Rathway stepped from his place of seclusion as though satisfied, lighted a cigar, and walked down the street.

"I'll just keep my eye on that man!" Brown told himself. "Yes, I'll do just that!"

CHAPTER XV

L ORENZO BRAYTON was in excellent spirits the following morning as he began going through his mail, his stenographer sitting beside him with pencil and notebook ready. Among the letters was one with a Newark postmark, and in the upper corner the business card of a certain Martin Cogblen, with whom Brayton had had shady dealings several times before. Cogblen was a man supposedly of sterling character, and so far as his own office was concerned he was all of that. He was honesty itself in small deals that served to gain him a reputation, but he indulged in side lines now and then.

Cogblen was the sort of man who "steered" a good thing in the direction of Lorenzo Brayton and then sat back and reaped a small portion of the reward. The association was remunerative to Brayton, for Cogblen picked men with money and no brains.

It was with deep interest, then, that Brayton ripped Cogblen's letter open and read it:

DEAR BRAYTON: I have been doing some business for a certain gentleman named John Gordon Wattler, a man of means and wide commercial connections. He has something in mind that is too large for me to handle and needs a man like you, who can be in touch with financial centers. Mr. Wattler is an extremely busy man, and is compelled to go West in two days regarding a mining venture, but I have persuaded him to see you first.

He will run over to the city Thursday evening, and hopes to find you in your office about ten o'clock. If you take a fancy to the affair, he will remain with you until you have completed arrangements, all night if necessary, so have a notary you can call. The business is of such a nature that he will want to speak to you alone regarding it. I trust that I make myself clear?

In addition, I am forwarding in your care, addressed to Mr. Wattler, a package that he wants to be there when he arrives. Take good care of it until he comes; I am not sure, but I think there are ore samples in it. Do not allow your curiosity to run away with you, for Wattler is a peculiar man in some things. I'd advise that you keep the engagement—and kindly remember me if anything comes of it.

Martin Cogblen had signed the letter by typewriter, but beneath the signature was an initial in ink that convinced Brayton the letter was genuine.

Brayton leaned back in his chair and smiled after he had read the letter a second time. It was plain enough. John Gordon Wattler had a scheme that he wanted a man with nerve to handle. And he was in a rush—probably had several schemes under way. Well, Lorenzo Brayton would be in the office at ten o'clock that night, and he would meet Wattler half way!

Brayton continued the perusal of his mail and drafted a form letter concerning the stock of an oil company. Within an hour the package was delivered. Brayton looked it over carefully. It was about a cubic foot, and fairly heavy, wrapped in heavy express paper and sealed in half a score of places.

Brayton grinned and put the package on the top of his desk, to remain there until Mr. Wattler's visit.

"Ore samples, eh?" Brayton said. "The time is about ripe for another big mining game. I only hope that it is copper. It takes time to develop a copper property—and time means money."

At the same time, in his office on the floor above, Peter Satchley was reading a letter purporting to be from Martin Cogblen, of Newark, with evident satisfaction.

DEAR MR. SATCHLEY: I have something in mind that calls for a man of your skill and financial knowledge; something which should be profitable in the extreme. I am running out into the country on some minor business, but hope to be in the city on Thursday evening. Suppose I call at your office at about ten o'clock, so that we can hold a conference without fear of being interrupted. I am writing you because I have heard some things recently that convince me Brayton is "in bad" and could not handle this deal to advantage.

Satchley grinned as he finished the letter. He knew all about Martin Cogblen, and undoubtedly Cogblen had something good in view. He was gratified that Cogblen was coming to him instead of going to Brayton. Certainly he would be in his office at ten o'clock.

There was nothing to indicate that tragedy hung over the building, unless it was the presence of Detective Sam Haynes, who spent a great deal of time around the corner and in the lobby at the cigar store.

Madame Violette was enjoying excellent business, and Madame Moonshine was having a special sale of blouses, in an effort to get enough ready money to discount some bills. Brown was trying to unload some atrocious cravats sent him by mistake from a wholesale house. But Brown was watching the stairs, and when Margaret Dranger came down them on her way to luncheon around the corner, he confronted her.

"Did you get your purse?" he asked.

"Yes, thank you," she replied, smiling at him. "Mrs. Murphy gave it to me this morning."

"I didn't take it up to the house until about ten o'clock," Brown said.

"That's all right. I thought I'd left it in the beauty parlor. I'm sorry I didn't see you last night to thank you, but I was tired and had gone to bed."

"Went to bed early?" Brown gasped.

"At about eight o'clock. Isn't that terrible, in New York?"

Brown scratched at his left ear again after she had gone. Margaret Dranger, for some reason, had told him a falsehood. Mrs. Murphy, too, certainly had lied the evening before.

"None of my business, I suppose," Brown grumbled. "Looks mighty funny to me, though. And that Rathway man watching her——"

Late in the afternoon Rathway entered Brown's shop and stated that he wished to purchase a shirt and wanted Brown to wait on him, as he was fastidious about shirts and usually looked at two dozen before he bought one. Brown guessed that Rathway was laying the foundation for a long, rambling talk, during which he would ask a multitude of questions, and he guessed correctly.

"That fellow Brayton stung almost everybody around the building, didn't he?" Rathway asked.

"He stung me, at least," Brown replied. "I suppose that there were plenty of others."

"Seems to me there should be some way of getting at him," Rathway declared.

"My lawyer says there isn't, and he is a good lawyer."

"Oh, I suppose he couldn't be touched in court— but there may be other ways," Rathway said. "If I were in your place, believe me I'd beat him up or something!"

"And be fined a hundred dollars," Brown muttered. "He has cost me enough money as it is. It'd be worth a hundred to beat him up—but I can't spare the hundred."

"I've been looking for Madame Violette's son to go after him," Rathway said. "That boy hasn't forgotten, you can bet your life! I wouldn't want him feeling toward me as he does toward Brayton. Murder is in his face."

"Nonsense!" Brown exclaimed. "Seems to me you take a lot of interest in the thing. Brayton didn't get any of your money, did he?"

"He certainly did not. The thing blew up before I got well enough acquainted with him."

"Well, you should be thankful, then," Brown said. "You'll take this shirt?"

"Wrap it up," Rathway instructed, fumbling in his waistcoat pocket for some money. "I've taken an interest just because I hate to see people robbed. Then, if I'm going to have an office in the building, I want to be one of the family, of course."

Brown handed him the shirt and gave him his change.

"That's a funny little girl Madame Violette has with her now," Rathway offered.

"Which one?"

"Miss Dranger," Rathway said. "I notice you've been looking at her a bit."

"She seems to be a very nice young lady," Brown told him, feeling a little anger.

"Oh, she's nice enough, I guess. But she acts a bit peculiar at times. Came from Chicago, I understand. Funny how she landed a job here so soon, and with Madame Violette."

"I don't see anything peculiar about that. She went to Mrs. Murphy's boarding house; Mrs. Murphy knows Madame Violette and knew that she wanted another girl, so she sent Miss Dranger there, and she got the job. You worry a lot about other persons."

Rathway grinned. "I usually know what I'm doing, Brown. See you again when I need anything in your line."

CHAPTER XVI

AT ten o'clock that night Lorenzo Brayton sat before the desk in his private office awaiting the arrival of John Gordon Wattler.

Brayton had closed the door that led to the front office, allowing the lights in front to burn. He wanted Wattler to think that he had found Lorenzo Brayton engrossed in work.

Brayton lighted a cigar now and leaned back in his desk chair, listening for the opening of the corridor door. Ten minutes passed, and nobody came.

"Hope he doesn't keep me waiting here until midnight," Brayton growled.

He glanced toward the closed door—and saw the knob begin to turn. There was something almost mysterious about that silent turning of the knob, as though it were being done by supernatural fingers. Brayton watched it, fascinated, while fear gripped him. He seemed to be unable to get out of his chair. He remembered suddenly that he did not have a weapon in the office, and he cursed himself for not having his bodyguard near.

Then the door opened an inch or so, and Brayton tried to tell himself that it was the janitor looking in to make sure that the lights had not been left burning by mistake, or else a watchman grown suspicious and wanting to ascertain whether thieves were at work.

The door opened another six inches, and Brayton caught a glimpse of scarlet cloth. Through his brain flashed remembrance of the letter he had received, signed by The Scarlet Scourge. Was it a trick? Had the letter from Cogblen been a trick? Was Wattler a menace instead of a business associate?

Then the door was thrown wide open, and Brayton half sprang from his chair. He no longer was alone in the private office. Another person had entered, and the door had been closed and locked.

And such a person! Brayton's eyes almost bulged from his head. The figure was clothed in a long scarlet robe, so long that Brayton could not even see the shoes. Over the head was a hood of the same material. The hands were covered with scarlet gloves. Nothing of the person inside the costume showed except the eyes—and not much of those. They gleamed through two tiny slits that were so narrow Brayton could not even make out what color they were.

"What—what!" he gasped.

The Scarlet Scourge signaled for silence and stepped closer to the desk. In one hand this menace held an automatic pistol, and its muzzle covered Brayton's heart. The other hand dived into a pocket of the scarlet robe and brought forth a pack of cards about four inches long and three wide. One of these cards was tossed before Lorenzo Brayton on the desk.   On it a single word was printed in red: "Silence."

Brayton tossed the card aside and wet his dry lips with his tongue.   He glanced up and encountered the glittering eyes.   He looked at the automatic pistol again, and a shudder ran through his frame.

Was this some man or woman he had swindled who had come to take an awful revenge?   Brayton knew that he could not tell whether it was a man or a woman.   The scarlet robe and hood and gloves covered everything, and as yet The Scarlet Scourge had not spoken a word.

"Who are you?   What do you want?" he gasped.

The Scarlet Scourge pointed to the card by way of reminder, and Brayton feared to speak again. The figure seemed to him to represent blood, death, oblivion!   There was silence for a moment, save for Brayton's heavy breathing, and then The Scarlet Scourge stepped forward another pace and tossed another card on the desk.   Brayton picked it up and read:

Do as I say unless you wish to die imme- diately.   Get out your check book and write a check for ten thousand dollars, payable to The Scarlet Scourge.

Brayton read the thing and then looked up in surprise.   He almost grinned despite his fear.

"You'll never be able to cash it, you fool!" he said.

Once more The Scarlet Scourge pointed to the

card that demanded silence, and at the same time
the automatic was moved a trifle. That move
was enough to strike fear into the heart of Lorenzo
Brayton once more. He glanced up at his peculiar
visitor. Something seemed to tell him now that
the letter from Cogblen was a hoax. Or was this
apparition in scarlet the man Wattlers, and was
he but playing some sort of game?

"I've had about enough of this nonsense!" Brayton exclaimed. "If you've had your fun——"

The Scarlet Scourge stepped nearer and bent
forward. Lorenzo Brayton found himself held spell-
bound by those two glittering eyes. Again fear
surged into his heart, a fear that he could not
understand. He gulped, licked at his lips again,
and his hands, spread out before him on the desk,
trembled.

The Scarlet Scourge pointed to his desk, and
Brayton opened a drawer and took out his check
book. He wrote the check for ten thousand, payable to The Scarlet Scourge, and with a shaking
hand affixed his signature.

Surely, he thought, this must be a joke of some
sort, and yet he did not feel that it was a joke.
Anybody, even the worst fool in the world, would
know that a check made out to such a payee could
not be cashed at any reputable bank. Of course,
that name might be erased and another substituted
over his signature. But, if that was the intention,
why was he not forced to make out a check payable
to "Cash?"

The Scarlet Scourge stepped closer and held out

a hand, and Brayton put the check in it. Again he looked up into those glittering eyes, again he tried to decide whether this menace was a man or a woman. The printed cards were new things—they made it impossible for Brayton to hear a voice and so form an opinion. Despite his fear, he realized the cleverness of the idea. What could he say afterward that would aid officers of the law, if he wished to call them in? Nothing except that his visitor seemed to be about five feet five or six inches tall.

He tried to convince himself that the whole thing was a joke, and almost succeeded. He did not think that he was being robbed, since the check had such a peculiar payee. Was this some game put up by Satchley just to make a fool of him? He had swindled Satchley out of an even ten thousand dollars, and the fact that The Scarlet Scourge had the check made out for that amount looked suspicious.

Now his visitor stepped close to the desk once more and tossed another card printed in red ink on the blotter before Brayton. He bent and read it:

Open the package addressed to John Gordon Wattler and sent in your care.

Brayton looked up quickly. Was it a joke after all, some scheme of this fellow Wattler? He reached to the top of the desk and took down the package and opened it.

Before him on the desk was a highly polished

wooden box about ten cubic inches in size. Brayton
glanced at it and looked up at The Scarlet Scourge
in surprise, to meet again those glittering eyes,
whose malevolent gleam frightened him. The Scarlet
Scourge motioned for him to open the box, and
Brayton turned the catch and lifted the lid. He
saw an electric battery.

Now The Scarlet Scourge stepped forward again
and tossed another card on the desk, and Lorenzo
Brayton read his further instructions:

You will grasp the handles of the battery,
and then I shall leave you. For five minutes
I shall be watching and listening. If you make
a sound in that time your life will be forfeit.
Do not doubt that I mean business.

Again Brayton met those glittering eyes, and
then The Scarlet Scourge motioned for him to do
as he had been directed. He shivered as he put
out his hands and grasped the battery handles.
Immediately it seemed that a million red-hot needles
were jabbing him along the arms and up and down
the spine. He twisted and writhed, tried to let
go of the battery handles and could not, and looked
up again to find that The Scarlet Scourge was
backing to the door, but still holding the automatic
ready for instant use.

The perspiration stood out on Lorenzo Brayton's
forehead. He wanted to shout for help, but did
not dare. He seemed to sense that The Scarlet
Scourge would shoot at the slightest provocation.

His tormentor darted into the outer office and closed the door and locked it. Brayton noticed that the lights in the outer office were extinguished immediately. Now he struggled desperately to be free, but found that he could not let go of the handles. The current was flowing through his body—not enough to kill nor to harm to any great extent, but enough to hold him prisoner and cause him agony.

He wondered whether The Scarlet Scourge was in the outer office, listening. He tried to decide how long it had been since his tormentor had left, whether the five minutes were at an end yet.

Again he tried ineffectually to shake off the battery handles. Instead, he gripped them the harder. Pains seemed to be shooting up and down his arms now, along his spine, down into his legs. He felt that he could endure the torture no longer.

He jerked the battery off the desk, but could not release the handles. He tried to reach the lever with his foot and throw off the current, but could not do that because the lever was held with a spring.

He wanted to scream, yet he was afraid to do so. Perhaps The Scarlet Scourge had left the office and the building—but, on the other hand, The Scarlet Scourge might be just on the other side of the door, ready to rush in and fire a fatal shot.

He told himself that he could not remain quiet much longer. The agony of the electric current was all that he could endure. He did not consider now whether this was a jest, did not stop to think what The Scarlet Scourge might do with the peculiar check he had written.

Another moment he waited—a moment that seemed an age. Then he could endure his torment no longer. He shouted for help!

CHAPTER XVII

THAT night, at the hour of ten, Peter Satchley also smoked and sat before his desk, waiting for the visit of Mr. Martin Cogblen and what it might bring forth. He hoped that it might be something unusually good, for he wanted to undertake a gigantic enterprise that would result in a huge profit. Afterward he meant to inform Lorenzo Brayton of what he had done.

Thought of Brayton brought a flush of anger to Satchley's face. He had been endeavoring to get the man out of his mind for several days, promising to punish him later, but found that he could not. The will to take Brayton's throat in his gripping hands was strong in Satchley. He was the sort of man who needs only a motive and an opportunity to become a cold-blooded murderer.

He heard distant chimes strike the hour of ten, and he smoked and waited, wondering what sort of scheme Cogblen would have and whether it would be highly profitable. Fifteen minutes passed. Satchley picked up an evening paper and began reading the news. He supposed that Cogblen had been delayed, that the train was late or something like that.

Then there came the sharp click of a knob turned,

the door was opened, and Satchley looked up to greet his man. Instead, his jaw sagged and his cigar dropped to the rug. Before him was The Scarlet Scourge.

"Wh-what——" Satchley began.

Then he saw that the apparition in red held an automatic in a menacing fashion, and he saw, too, the eyes that glittered through the mask. They struck terror to his heart even as they had to the heart of Lorenzo Brayton.

Step by step the scarlet apparition approached him. Satchley felt as though glued to his chair. He was gripping the edge of the desk so that his knuckles were white, while he tried to find voice and was unable to do so.

A card was tossed before him. He read:

Silence. A move or a word and it will mean the end of you, you grafter.

In that instant through the mind of Satchley there flashed quick portraits of the men and women he had swindled while in partnership with Brayton. He knew that it was not Brayton in the red robe, for Brayton was a giant of a man, and this being was of medium size. His quick wit was at work, too, and he convinced himself almost instantly that he could not swear whether this person were man or woman, fat or thin, blond or brunet. He was as puzzled as Brayton had been; more so, for Brayton had received a warning regarding The Scarlet Scourge, and Peter Satchley had not.

Now another card was tossed before him, and he read it swiftly, hoping for a solution of the mystery:

I am called The Scarlet Scourge. Do as I direct and your life is not in danger. Refuse, and you die instantly.

"What—what do you wish me to do?" Satchley stammered.

The Scarlet Scourge stepped forward quickly. One scarlet finger pointed to the first card, which demanded silence. Satchley, suddenly weak, sank back in his chair. Another card was placed before him. The red printing on this was much smaller. Satchley read it:

I have a check I want you to cash for me immediately. It is properly made out, the signature is genuine, and the check is indorsed. It was written by a man with whom you have had many business dealings. The least hesitation on your part will be punished. If you have to speak, do so in a whisper.

Peter Satchley looked up and nodded to signify that he understood. The check was put before him on the desk, and he picked it up at once and inspected it.

He saw instantly that it was for ten thousand dollars, made out in favor of The Scarlet Scourge, and signed by Lorenzo Brayton. It was Brayton's signature, he knew.   He knew also that he never would get his money back if he cashed the check. Either this was a game of Brayton's, or else some enemy of them both was trying to collect from them.

"The check's—no good," he said.

He anticipated hearing the voice of the scarlet apparition, but was disappointed.   Another card was tossed before him.   Satchley read it:

No argument. The check was written properly and the signature is genuine. If you cannot cash it later, that will be no fault of mine. I am not inclined to waste time. Cash it instantly.

Satchley looked up again, and once more he whispered:

"I haven't that amount of money with me here, as you might know," he said.   "You're working a bum game; you're up against a stone wall.   Do you think I carry as much coin as that in my waistcoat pocket?"

The Scarlet Scourge tossed another card on the desk.   Satchley marveled that the apparition had a card for almost every question, as though the victim's arguments had been anticipated.   It was almost uncanny.   This card convinced him that he was dealing with somebody who knew a great deal and would endure no delay.   He read it:

I happen to know that you keep what you call a "get-away stake" of ten thousand dollars in your safe. Cash this check at once; my patience is about exhausted. I need only an excuse for putting a bullet through you!

Peter Satchley was a coward at heart. Now he looked into the malevolent eyes once more, and realized that he was alone in his office with The Scarlet Scourge at a late hour at night, and that he was looking into the muzzle of an automatic of the most approved pattern.

At first he was inclined to resist, but he decided that it would be foolish and undoubtedly would result in disaster to himself. It was the fear of the unknown that gripped him, the uncertainty of the identity of The Scarlet Scourge. Had the person in the scarlet robe spoken it might have helped some, but Satchley had heard no word. There was something terrifying in the red costume, in that dread silence.

The perspiration standing out on his forehead, Peter Satchley rose weakly from his desk chair and walked across to his safe. He knelt before it and worked the combination, missing it the first time because of his nervousness. From an inner compartment of the safe he took a small bundle, and this he carried back to his desk.

He looked at The Scarlet Scourge now and then, but could detect no sign of weakness. Back at the desk he ripped the bundle open and tossed a package of bank notes out.

"It's there—just ten thousand," he whispered hoarsely.

The Scarlet Scourge bent forward and swept up the money with a red glove. The check was put down before Peter Satchley again.

"You can't—get away with this!" Satchley gasped. "I'll get you all——"

The moment he started to voice the threat, he grew horribly afraid. The Scarlet Scourge bent toward him again. Fascinated despite himself, Peter Satchley watched the muzzle of the automatic approach his forehead, inch by inch, and looked into those eyes that glittered through the slits in the mask. Satchley leaned back in the chair, gasping, the fear of violent death upon him. But the shot he had expected did not come. Instead, his unknown assailant put another of those peculiar cards before him. It read:

I am going to lock you in the little closet in the corner of your office.

Satchley looked up to see The Scarlet Scourge motioning in that direction. After an instant of hesitation, the swindler rose and crossed the room to the closet. He opened the door, which was a heavy one set in a strong frame, and stepped inside. He could not hope to attack or outwit this unknown being in the scarlet gown and mask, but he could hope to break out of the closet within a short time and give an alarm.

As he stepped inside he was handed another card. A single glance sufficed to read the message:

Make no sound for five minutes unless you wish to die.

The Scarlet Scourge closed the door slowly and carefully, and Peter Satchley, standing there in the darkness and heat, heard the key turned in the lock on the other side.

He strained his ears to catch any sound from the office, but could hear nothing. He wanted to be sure that his unknown enemy was gone before he attempted to break out of the closet.

There was a moment of silence, and then, from the distance, came cries and shrieks—calls for help!

CHAPTER XVIII

A HOMICIDE CASE

PETER SATCHLEY heard the shrieks and cries, and they struck terror to his heart, but he could not determine from whence they came. They ceased almost immediately, and again there was deep silence. In the stuffy closet, Satchley felt the perspiration streaming from his face and hands, fought to get his breath, and tried to conquer his fear enough to make a determined attack upon the strong door that barred the way to freedom.

He waited until he felt sure that at least ten minutes had passed, for he still felt the menace of The Scarlet Scourge; and then he threw his weight against the panels in front of him. The door groaned and shivered, but did not give way either at lock or hinges.

Although handicapped in the narrow space, Satchley hurled himself at the door repeatedly, until finally the wood around the lock cracked. Then he redoubled his efforts. The door gave a trifle, and a final lunge caused it to fly wide open. Satchley staggered into the office, fighting for breath, almost exhausted, and sank into the nearest chair.

He did not remain there long, but, waiting only until he was breathing almost normally, sprang for his hat, which was on a rack in the corner of the room. A moment later the lights had been extinguished, the front door had been locked, and Peter Satchley was running down the corridor toward the elevators.

He pressed the button, rang the bell furiously, maintained a continuous ringing of it until he saw that one of the elevators had started up. It seemed to him that it never had been so slow before, but, as a matter of fact, it was one of the express elevators and was making excellent speed.

It stopped; the door was opened. Peter Satchley found himself looking into the face of old Frand.

"Been robbed!" Satchley gasped. "Get me down quick!"

Frand already had started the elevator downward.

"Robbed, you say?" he asked.

"Yes. Somebody dressed in a red robe, with a red mask and gloves. Made me hand over ten thousand in cash. Anybody go out just now?"

"No, sir. I've been sitting in front of the elevators," the janitor replied. "It's my night to be on duty, sir. Nobody has gone out or come in for a couple of hours or so."

"But I tell you——"

"It doesn't make any difference," Frand went on. "There are a dozen ways to get in and out of the building. There's a side entrance and a rear entrance, and a man could get through a window and onto the roof of the building to the west."

They reached the lower floor, and Satchley darted through the lobby to the doorway. Far down the street two pedestrians were talking together, the loud laughter of one of them ringing out. Just young men on their way home, Satchley supposed. And around the nearest corner came a police officer.

Satchley shouted at him, and the patrolman hurried forward to the entrance of the building.

"Robbed of ten thousand in my office a few minutes ago," Satchley gasped. "Robber was dressed in scarlet robe, red mask and gloves—used printed cards and never spoke a word. Locked me in closet; it took me some time to get out. This is Frand—janitor. Officer, I wish you'd stay here and grab anybody leaving the building. Frand knows all the regular tenants. I'll go to the nearest police station and get a detective."

The officer nodded, and Satchley hurried out to the curb. Luck was with him, for an empty taxicab came around the corner, and the chauffeur answered his frantic signaling. An instant later Peter Satchley was on his way to the nearest police station.

He told his story there in a few words. The captain in charge assigned two plain-clothes men to the case. They hurried back with Satchley in the taxicab, and Frand took them up in the elevator, while the patrolman remained on duty in the lobby.

Again Peter Satchley told the story of what had happened to him. He showed the officers the cards that The Scarlet Scourge had left.

"How does it happen that you had such an amount of money in your safe?" he was asked.

"I always keep ten thousand there, in case I

should need funds out of banking hours for the purchase of securities," Satchley explained quickly.

"But how did the thief know that?"

"That is what puzzles me," Satchley declared. "Even my stenographer didn't know it. I had the currency in a little package and kept it in the inner compartment of the safe. The thief knew of it; told me of it when I tried to evade him by saying that I didn't have much cash on me."

"Well, who could have known about it?" Satchley was asked.

"Lorenzo Brayton, a broker with offices in this building, knew of it," Satchley replied. "Formerly I was his partner, but we ended our friendship recently when I discovered that he was a crook. He swindled me. I understand he has had trouble with others in this building."

"Think it was Brayton in the scarlet robe?"

"No, it was not. Brayton is a huge man, and this person was of medium size. Whether it was somebody Brayton sent, I do not know, of course."

"How did it happen you were in the office so late?"

"I received a letter from a Mr. Martin Cogblen, of Newark, a gentleman with whom I have business relations occasionally. He asked me to be in the office about ten o'clock, said that he would be in town and wanted to see me about something important. There is nothing unusual in that. I was here waiting for him."

"Any reason why this Cogblen should want to rob you?"

"Heavens, no! We are on excellent terms, both in a business and a social way," Satchley replied.

"But he didn't show up?"

"He did not," Satchley admitted. "Perhaps he missed his train. You can find out about that in the morning, of course."

"Looks funny," one of the officers declared. "You sure nobody but Brayton knew about that ten thousand?"

"I know of nobody else who could have been aware of it," Satchley said. "Brayton used to keep such a fund in his own safe, but he told me recently that he had transferred it to a hotel safe, where he could get it if he needed it."

"Well, that was a wise move," the officer replied. "I think we'd better get in touch with Brayton. We'll tell him that there has been a thief at work in the building, and that perhaps he'd better come down and look his office over. Then we can talk to him. That's all we want."

Brayton's apartment was called, and the Japanese servant replied that Mr. Brayton was not there, that he had left soon after dinner and had said that he was going to the office for a business conference.

"He may be in his office now," Satchley said. "It is on the floor below, almost directly beneath this one."

"We'll go there," one of the officers declared.

Satchley accompanied them. They went down the stairs and along the hall, and came to Brayton's suite. There was no light in the front office, but the glare through the ground-glass doors showed that one was burning in the private office.

Satchley hung back, while the two officers walked into the front office, approached the door to the private room, and knocked.   There was no reply. The door was unlocked and thrown open.   Peter Satchley, standing in the corridor, heard one of the officers speak.

"Mr. Brayton!   Asleep, sir?"

Then there was silence for an instant, and then an exclamation of surprise. Satchley glanced through the door and saw the officers rushing into the private office.   He followed, but stopped just inside the doorway.

Brayton was in the desk chair, his head bowed forward upon his hands, which were sprawled on the desk before him.   One of the officers was making a swift examination.

"Dead!" he reported.

"What!" Satchley exclaimed.

"Dead," the officer replied.   "Shot through the back as he sat at his desk.   Here's a job for the homicide squad!"

And so Detective Sam Haynes found himself ordered to Brayton's office, and became firmly convinced that certain officers can "feel a crime coming."

CHAPTER XIX

ONE VIEW OF IT

YAWNING and bewailing the fortune that had pulled him out of bed within half an hour after he had managed to get to sleep, Detective Sam Haynes reached Brayton's office to find Satchley and the two plain-clothes men sitting in the front room awaiting him. Frand had brought him up in the elevator—a white-faced Frand, who seemed about to go to pieces in face of the tragedy.

"Notified the medical examiner?" Haynes asked as soon as he entered the room.

"Yes," one of the plain-clothes men replied. "Here is one of his assistants now."

The assistant entered and made a quick examination of the body. He stated that death had been almost instantaneous, and had resulted from a single bullet wound. Then he went away to make his report to his superior, and the body was removed.

Detective Sam Haynes was left in charge of operations. He walked slowly around the private office and made a minute investigation while the others remained in the outer room. Beneath the desk chair, where Brayton had been sitting, was a pool of blood. On the top of the desk was an electric battery such as some ill men use. The door of the safe was open, and there were some papers scattered about the floor. One of the filing-case drawers had been pulled out and dumped in a corner. There were no signs of a life-and-death struggle.

"Um!" Haynes grunted. "Murder and robbery without a doubt. And some interesting angles to the case, or I miss my guess."

He walked back into the front office and sat down. Peter Satchley, his face white, was sitting within four feet of him. Detective Sam Haynes regarded him carefully.

"I want to hear your story, Satchley," he said. "There may be some connection between your experience and this matter, you see."

Satchley told it quickly—about receiving the letter, about the visit of The Scarlet Scourge, about cashing the check, about being locked in the closet, and about how he made his escape and gave the alarm. Haynes questioned him carefully, and then left the office for a time and had a short talk with old Frand, the janitor.

When he returned and sat down again, there was a peculiar expression in Haynes' face.

"Nobody seems to have seen this Scarlet Scourge except you, Mr. Satchley," he said. "It is peculiar how the thief knew about that ten thousand dollars in your safe. You are sure that Brayton was not The Scarlet Scourge?"

"I am certain of it. Brayton was a giant of a man, as you know, and the thief was only of medium size."

Haynes got up and went into the inner office

again, and for a time he searched the papers on Brayton's desk. When he returned he had two letters in his hand.

"Here is a note from this Scarlet Scourge," Haynes reported. "And here are some cards similar to those which Satchley says The Scarlet Scourge left with him. Moreover, here is something interesting. It is a letter from Martin Cogblen."

"From Cogblen?" Satchley asked.

"It tells Brayton to be in his office to-night at ten o'clock, and says that a man named John Gordon Wattler will call to see him about business. Know this Wattler?"

"Never heard the name before."

"The letter also mentions a package that Wattler was sending, addressed to himself, in Brayton's care, and says to hold it for Wattler's arrival. Here is the wrapper of the package. Since it was in a corner, it must have been taken off to-night— after the regular visit of the floor janitor, in other words. Possibly it was removed after Brayton came to the office."

"But the package?" Satchley asked.

"See that electric battery? The paper wrappings fit it and show that they were around it. The battery was in the package. But Brayton was not electrocuted; he was shot. That battery might make a man uncomfortable, but it never would kill him."

"Then this Wattler——" Satchley began.

"If Wattler visited Brayton, we want to talk to him," Haynes declared, "and ask him several pointed questions. And we want to ascertain why Martin Cogblen wrote those letters, and why he didn't visit your office, Satchley, as he said he would do. Were you on good terms with Brayton?"

"Not exactly," Satchley said. "We were business associates, in a way, for years, but recently we parted company. I did not admire his business methods. Not long ago he swindled me out of ten thousand dollars, and I told him that I was done with him."

"Um!" Haynes grunted. "You are frank, and that is a good thing. You were inclined to have revenge, weren't you?"

"Naturally. But I wanted to hit him in the purse, not shoot him in the back."

"I'm not intimating that you shot him, Satchley. I'm merely gathering information," Haynes told him. "Did you think Brayton was responsible for the robbery to-night?"

"I scarcely knew. Of course it looked peculiar, since he was the only person, so far as I knew, who was aware of the ten thousand dollars in my safe. It flashed through my mind that perhaps he had hired somebody to play the trick."

Detective Sam Haynes went into the private office again, sat down at the desk before the telephone, and put in a call for Martin Cogblen at Newark, giving the operator his name and requesting that the call be rushed.

It was ten minutes before the telephone buzzer sounded, and Haynes spent that time pacing the floor of the office, evidently deep in thought. When the call came, he removed the receiver and put it to his left ear.

"Mr. Cogblen?" he asked.

"Yes."

"This is Detective Sam Haynes, of the New York police department, speaking.   I am in the office of Lorenzo Brayton."

"Yes?"

"I want to ask you a few questions, Mr. Cogblen. Did you intend coming over to the city to-night?"

"Far from it," Cogblen replied.   "I've been confined to my home for three days with a terrible cold. It's better now, but my doctor has ordered me to remain indoors for the remainder of the week."

"Um!" Haynes grunted.   "Didn't you write a letter to Mr. Satchley telling him you wished to see him in his office at ten o'clock this evening?"

"I certainly did not.   I haven't written a letter to Satchley for a couple of weeks."

"Do you know a man named Wattler?"

"Never heard the name," Cogblen said.   "What's the trouble, anyway?"

"Mr. Brayton received a letter purporting to have come from you, saying that Mr. Wattler would visit him to-night at his office on business.   The letter also mentioned a package sent in care of Brayton for Wattler."

"I don't know anything about it," Cogblen said.

"The letter was written on one of your letterheads and inclosed in one of your envelopes."

"Signed by me?"

"Signed on the typewriter, with an initial beneath

the signature.   Mr. Satchley also had a letter on one of your letterheads, saying that you wanted to see him to-night."

"I don't know anything about that, either," Cogblen replied.   "I didn't write either of the letters. I wish you'd bring them over and let me see them."

"I'll send them over in the morning," Haynes promised.   "I guess that's all I care to ask you now, Mr. Cogblen."

"But what happened?"

"Mr. Brayton has been found in his office, shot; he is dead," Haynes reported.

"Good heavens!"

"I'll send the letters," Haynes said, and rang off.

The detective walked back into the front office and looked at Peter Satchley again.

"Cogblen is sick and in his home, and he says that he never wrote those letters or sent that package," he reported.   "I'll investigate further, of course, but I am inclined now to believe that he spoke the truth.   Do you know what some detectives would say at this juncture, Satchley?   They would declare that you shot Lorenzo Brayton."

"That I shot him!"

"Sure The Scarlet Scourge wasn't a myth?"

"Great heavens, man," Satchley cried, "I tell you that I was robbed of ten thousand dollars!"

"How do I know that you had ten thousand in the safe?   I'm just telling you what some detectives would think, Satchley.   They'd say that, if The Scarlet Scourge existed——"

"There are the cards that——"

"Yes, and the letter printed in red, but you might have arranged for those, Satchley. As I was saying, some detectives might think that you did have a visit from The Scarlet Scourge, that you thought Brayton had sent the fellow to rob you, that you went immediately to Brayton's office as soon as you got out of that closet, shot him, ransacked the desk and filing case for your ten thousand, then hurried back to your own office, or down in the elevator, and gave the alarm that you had been robbed."

"You're insane, man!"

"Oh, no—just speculating a bit," Haynes answered. "Some detectives might say that there was no Scarlet Scourge except a myth of your own invention, that you had sent the letters, decoyed Brayton to his office, shot him, and then scattered those cards around. He swindled you out of ten thousand recently, you said."

"I—I never did it!" Satchley gasped.

"That's all right," Haynes said. "Go on home, Satchley, and try to calm yourself."

Satchley went. Detective Haynes made a motion, and one of the plain-clothes men disappeared also. Whether he guessed it or not, Peter Satchley was under surveillance.

CHAPTER XX

MR. RATHWAY ASSISTS

DETECTIVE SAM HAYNES dismissed the other plain-clothes man after a time, and then locked the front door of Lorenzo Brayton's office suite and went into the private room.

Slowly and carefully he went over the room, inspecting the papers first that had been spilled from the filing case, and putting them back in their regular places, trying to ascertain whether any were missing. But the case had not been more than two thirds filled, and he couldn't determine this.

He examined the safe again. He smoked as he worked, and now and then whistled beneath his breath. The inner compartment of the safe was open and empty, but it had not been forced open. Neither was the combination damaged. In one corner was a fireproof filing case with an intricate lock, and this was unlocked and open an inch or so, but that, too, had not been forced.

The contents had been taken from Brayton's pockets. Haynes picked up the bunch of keys and soon discovered that those which unlocked the filing case and the inner compartment of the safe were on the ring. If the murderer had used those keys, he had taken them from the dead man's pocket, unlocked the locks and then returned the keys. That did not seem probable.

Then Haynes stood back by the door and regarded the chair in which the dead body of Lorenzo Brayton had been found. Sitting in that chair, Brayton would have had his back toward the door that led to the front office. Also, a man standing in the door that opened into the corridor could have fired a shot that would have pierced Brayton's back toward one side. If Brayton had been sitting at his desk when the shot was fired, as it appeared, the murderer could have been in either doorway.

A silencer could have been used on the weapon, of course. But the guilty man must have been a cool one to have rifled the safe and filing cases after committing the crime.

"I'll bet that he never used Brayton's keys," Haynes mused. "He had keys, and he knew the combination of the safe—unless it happened that Brayton had the safe open at the time. Well, the man had enemies enough."

He continued his investigation, received several newspaper men, and finally closed and locked the office and went to the elevator. He pressed the buzzer, and old Frand brought up the car.

Haynes said nothing as he rode to the ground floor, but when it was reached, he engaged Frand in conversation.

"Don't let anybody fuss around that office," Haynes instructed. "I'll be here before Brayton's stenographer and office boy arrive in the morning."

"I—I understand, sir," old Frand said.

"What time did you take Brayton to his office?"

"I didn't take him up, sir. I came on duty at

ten o'clock, exactly. The man who attends to the night elevator always comes on duty then, sir, and remains until six in the morning, and then has the following day off."

"I see. What time was it when Mr. Peter Satchley came into the building?"

"I don't know, sir. I didn't know that he was in the building until he rang for the elevator and I brought him down. He told me that he had been robbed. He signaled a policeman, and the officer stood here in the lobby until Mr. Satchley returned from the station with two officers in plain clothes."

"Who went in or came out?"

"Nobody, sir, except a gentleman who has an office on the third floor. He came in about five minutes before Mr. Satchley rang for the elevator, sir."

"Stay long?"

"Oh, no, sir. He just darted into his office, which is almost opposite the elevator, sir. He told me to wait for him, and I did. He got some papers, hurried right out again, and I took him down and he went away. It was Mr. Jones, sir, the attorney."

"Nobody else came in or went out?"

"Not through the lobby, sir; I would have seen them. I didn't run the car down into the basement, and when it is hot like this and there is no work to be done, I sit on that stool before the elevator."

"Somebody might have come in or gone out while you were taking Jones up and bringing him down?"

"Yes, sir. That would have been the only time.

But it wasn't more than five minutes, sir. The— the murderer might have come in then, of course, sir. And, of course, he could have left the building in some other way—over the next roof, for instance."

"I understand. Brayton had a lot of enemies, I guess."

"I don't know about that, sir."

"He swindled some people, didn't he?"

"I—I think that he did, sir. He—he got all my savings," old Frand said, tears in his voice.

"How is that?"

"He persuaded me to invest in that rubber concern, sir, and I put in all my savings. It was a big blow to me when I found that the scheme was no good and my money was gone. I'm an old man, sir, and what I'll do when I can work no longer is more than I know."

Frand blinked his eyes rapidly to keep back the tears, but did not succeed entirely. Detective Sam Haynes felt sudden animosity against the man who had been slain, but he did not show it. Lorenzo Brayton might have been the greatest scoundrel on earth, but if he had been murdered it was Sam Haynes' duty to find the murderer and let him answer to the law.

He considered Frand as he walked down the street. Frand had a motive, and he certainly had had an opportunity to commit the murder. Had he been aware that Brayton was in his office, Frand could have gone up in the elevator, opened the corridor door with his janitor's key, fired the shot, and simply returned to the elevator and the ground floor again.

The news of the tragedy flashed through the building at an early hour next morning. The curious went to Brayton's office, to find that they could not get in, and that the officer there would not even let them loiter in the corridor.

"Served him right!" more than one person in the building said.

But those most concerned were careful in their attitudes and statements. Madame Violette went about her apartment with a peculiar expression on her face.

Madame Moonshine remained in her private office for a time, and when she emerged into the salesroom, there were traces of tears on her cheeks and in her eyes. She forbade her saleswomen and models to speak of the tragedy in the shop during working hours.

Brown, the haberdasher, went about his business as usual, except that there was a strained look in his face. He was cross with his clerks, too, and brusque in his dealings with customers. Madame Violette's son appeared distraught and nervous, but he had been that since the day he had discovered that Brayton's scheme was worthless and the funds intrusted to him gone forever.

Detective Sam Haynes, going through Lorenzo Brayton's papers, sought and found a list of those who had invested unwisely in the rubber corporation. He sat before the desk for some time, contemplating this list.   There were more than fifteen hundred subscribers to the stock issue, but Haynes decided to eliminate at first all those in other cities and in the rural districts.   He knew that the news of the company's failure had not traveled beyond the city.   It had not been in the newspapers!   In fact, only those in the vicinity of the building were aware of it.

Haynes made a list of those names in which he was interested, and slipped it into one of his pockets. It was only one angle of the case, of course.   There was a possibility that Brayton had been slain for revenge and that the murderer had robbed the safe; there also was the possibility that the crime was that of a professional criminal and for purposes of robbery only.   The fact that the murderer must have had the combination of the safe, and keys, gave color to the last hypothesis.

Haynes believed in The Scarlet Scourge.   He knew that Satchley and Brayton had been associated, and he thought that somebody in the guise of The Scarlet Scourge had forced Brayton to write the check, and then had demanded that Satchley cash it.   If that were the case, The Scarlet Scourge undoubtedly had slain Brayton.

The letters from Newark might have been decoys to get Brayton and Satchley in their offices at night.   But who would have known so much of their affairs?   Who would have known that Satchley kept ten thousand dollars in his safe?   And the safe combination?

There was a possibility, of course, that the safe already was unlocked when the murderer appeared; Brayton might have been looking at some papers he had taken from it. The murderer might have used Brayton's keys and returned them. Or possibly the strong box and the filing case were unlocked by Brayton, and the thief and murderer found everything ready for him.

About a quarter after nine o'clock the policeman ushered another man into the office.

"Insists upon seeing you, Haynes," the officer reported. "Says it is something about this case."

"My name's Rathway. I want to speak to you alone," the newcomer declared.

Haynes remembered seeing him in the building. He sent the policeman back to the corridor, and he and Rathway sat down.

"I've been posing as a manufacturer's agent, and have rented an office in this building," Rathway said. "As a matter of fact, I've been keeping an eye on Lorenzo Brayton. I'm with the government."

"Secret service?" Haynes asked.

"Yes. We've been on Brayton's trail for some time. He was a mighty smooth operator; I'll say that for him. We tried to get him in Chicago, where he was working with Peter Satchley, but we failed. Some time ago my chief assigned me to the case with orders to keep at it. Brayton was the sort of man to make a howl, and so we've been working in the dark, waiting until we had conclusive evidence before we made a move. I know a lot about the man and his dealings with other persons. Possibly I can help you."

"I'll be glad to have you," Haynes said. "I'm not given to professional jealousy."

"You get all the credit," Rathway explained. "The government doesn't appear in this officially, understand. Here is my badge—see? And kindly read this letter. If I work with you, you'll have to be governed by that letter, of course."

Detective Haynes read the letter at once. It was evident that Rathway had been carrying the document for some time; Haynes saw that it was dated almost three months before. The letter stated that the bearer, Morton Rathway, had been assigned to a special investigation of a secret nature and asked all peace officers to aid him in any way possible.

"Something that has to be kept quiet," Rathway explained. "Other men in the service do not even know what I've been doing. I've shown you my credentials. Please don't mention my standing to anybody else."

"All right," Haynes said. "I'll be glad if you can help me. Brayton was a scoundrel, I suppose, but if he was murdered——"

"Have to land his murderer—exactly," Rathway said. "He probably escaped a term in Atlanta prison by being killed. I was about ready to close in on him. I had planned to look over his papers when he wasn't around."

"Well, you can look over them now."

"Do no good now," Rathway declared. "Can't indict a dead man and send him to jail. I may discover something about certain other gentlemen, however."

"Peter Satchley, for instance?"

"Exactly," Rathway said. "Suppose you tell me, in a few words, what you have discovered. Then I'll know whether I have any information that will be of value to you."

Detective Sam Haynes complied, and after he had concluded Rathway got up and paced the floor.

"Well," he said finally, stopping before Haynes, "I am inclined to think that there really was a Scarlet Scourge—probably somebody who wanted to square accounts with both Brayton and Satchley. They used to be partners, and I suppose they have robbed many a man and woman in different parts of the country."

"No doubt of that," Haynes said.

"And the big question is, did The Scarlet Scourge do the murder? Brayton was found dead at his desk. The safe and file cases were open, you say. But the fact remains that Brayton wrote that check for ten thousand dollars. Satchley declares it is Brayton's writing and signature, and he ought to know. The check was dated yesterday. Seems to me that check was written last night, and that The Scarlet Scourge went from here directly to Satchley's office and forced him to cash it."

"That's the way it looks to me."

"And, so you say, Satchley says he heard shrieks when he was locked in the closet. That might mean that somebody came in here after The Scarlet Scourge left, and did the murder. Yet Brayton was found sitting at his desk, as though he had been shot in the back and had toppled forward. He wouldn't sit at his desk and yell. There were no signs of a fight?"

"No," Haynes answered. "There had been no struggle. It looks to me as though somebody had stepped to the door—either door—and had fired the shot."

"Thought about Satchley?"

"Yes," Haynes replied. "I've questioned Frand, the old janitor, about Satchley, too. I don't think he did it."

"What is your idea?"

"That The Scarlet Scourge did it—whoever The Scarlet Scourge may be," Haynes answered.

"It is my theory, at this time, that Brayton neglected his instructions and shrieked for help. Those were the cries Satchley says that he heard. According to Satchley, the cries ceased almost instantly."

"Well?"

"Don't you see? The Scarlet Scourge was still in the front office. He darted back and threatened Brayton, who ceased crying out for help. The Scarlet Scourge forced him to sit down and disconnected the battery. Then—a shot——"

"Why?"

"Because The Scarlet Scourge was in a hurry to make a get-away, and was afraid that Brayton would shout again the moment he was out of the room. So he shot Brayton in the back as the man sat at his desk."

"I believe you've hit it," Rathway said.

"But the rifled safe and filing cases puzzle me," Haynes admitted. "Those red printed cards say nothing about ordering Brayton to open the safe."

"I am assuming," said Rathway, "that while waiting for the visitor he expected, Brayton was attending to some business. He had the safe open, and the filing case, also. The Scarlet Scourge, in addition to forcing Brayton to write the check, robbed the open safe and possibly ran through the drawer of the filing case looking for valuables or to get a certain document. He could do it easily enough while Brayton held to the handles of the battery, and while the muzzle of a revolver was covering the victim."

"One thing is certain," Detective Sam Haynes declared, "when we find The Scarlet Scourge we'll know a lot about this."

CHAPTER XXI

INNOCENT OR CLEVER

AT a conference which Detective Sam Haynes held soon with his superior, Morton Rathway was present. Rathway was particular about some things; he was eager and willing to aid Haynes if it was in his power; but nobody was to know that he was doing so, or that he had been investigating Brayton's activities.

"You see, we're not done," he explained. "There are other wolves beside Brayton—a regular pack of them. If the news gets out that I have been trailing Brayton, some of the other wolves will make tracks."

He winked at Haynes and the chief, and the chief grinned by way of reply.

"I understand," he said.

"I am not to be mentioned at all," Rathway went on. "The department fell down once because the investigation was noised abroad. We don't want to fail this time; we want to land the men who are robbing women and old janitors, and such people as that. Nobody knows what I have been doing but my chief—not even my comrades in the service. And we don't want them to know. Understand? We don't want a leak."

"Nobody shall know," the chief promised.

It was decided that Haynes was to care for the Brayton case without any other assistant than Rathway, unless he called for help. Rathway and Haynes journeyed back toward the scene of the crime, conversing steadily.

"You go ahead on the lines we have laid down, Haynes," Rathway said. "I'm known around there merely as a manufacturer's agent who is opening an office in the building. Folks may talk before me when they wouldn't before you. If we meet we just barely know each other. I'll get out here, and you can go on alone; wouldn't do for us to be seen together right now."

Rathway left the taxicab at the corner, and Sam Haynes drove up to the building and got out. He turned into the haberdashery of George Brown and asked for the proprietor. Brown ushered him into the private office. The detective looked at the haberdasher narrowly. Brown seemed to be ill at ease. His face was pale, and there were dark hollows beneath his eyes.

"I'm investigating the Brayton murder," Haynes said. "I suppose you've heard of it?"

"Everybody has been talking about it. I haven't heard much else to-day," Brown said.

"I am interrogating the other tenants of the building," Haynes said. "Any way in which you can aid me?"

"How in Heaven's name could I help you solve a murder mystery?" George Brown asked.

"You knew Brayton, didn't you? I thought perhaps you may have seen some stranger talking to him, or overheard somebody quarreling with him."

"I tried to handle him myself a few days ago, as you know very well, since you helped separate us," Brown said.

"When did you see Brayton last?"

"I don't remember."

"Yesterday?"

"I'm not sure."

"Do you know anything about The Scarlet Scourge?"

Haynes watched Brown's face carefully as he spoke. But Brown betrayed no guilty emotion at mention of the name.

"Never heard of it!" he replied. "What's the joke?"

"It isn't a joke. Can you handle a typewriter?"

"I might carry it from one desk to another, if that's what you mean. I can't write on one," Brown answered.

"Do you own a revolver or firearm of any kind?"

"I have a revolver."

"May I see it?"

"Certainly," said Brown.

He got up and stepped across to a little table in one corner of his office. He pulled open a drawer, took out the weapon, and handed it to Haynes. The detective glanced at it and smiled. It was of an ancient pattern; coated with rust in places, its cylinder refused to revolve freely; it had not been used for some time.

"What time did you leave your store last night?" Haynes asked.

"About seven o'clock. I kept open until six—had a couple of customers after the clerks had gone. Then I attended to my books."

"And where did you go after you left the store?"

"To dinner at the restaurant around the corner. The head waiter can tell you that."

"And what time did you leave the restaurant?"

"About eight o'clock, I guess."

"And then?"

"Let me see. After leaving the restaurant I walked about for a time to cool off. It was mighty hot yesterday, and I had been working hard, unpacking new stock and helping wait on the trade after one of my clerks went home sick."

"Where did you walk?"

"Nowhere in particular."

"Meet anybody you knew?"

"I don't remember having done so," said Brown.

"Suppose you tell me, in your own words, where you were and what you were doing between eight o'clock and midnight last night," Haynes requested.

"I walked around—don't know how long—up one street and down another."

"For four hours?"

"Oh, I don't know exactly what I did. I didn't kill Brayton, at any rate."

"It will be to your interest to reply to my questions," Haynes warned him.

"I can't say any more."

"You mean that you will not?"

"Have it your own way," Brown told him.

"Don't you realize that this places you in a bad light?" the detective asked. "I know that it is a nuisance, submitting to an examination like this, but once I am satisfied, you will be let alone."

"I just walked around. I don't remember stopping in at any place."

"Didn't talk to anybody you knew?"

"Not a soul!"

"In all those four hours?"

"Not a soul!" Brown repeated.

"Very well, Brown. Now let's talk of something else. Have you heard anybody making threats against Lorenzo Brayton?"

"I heard Madame Moonshine say that she'd like to scratch his eyes out," Brown replied, chuckling a bit.

"I mean serious threats."

"Can't remember any," Brown said.

"Ever go to dances, Brown?"

"What do you mean by that?" Brown asked suddenly, sitting up straight in his chair, his eyes flashing.

"Nothing for you to storm about," Haynes said. "I merely asked whether you ever went to dances."

"I—I went to the haberdashers' ball the other night," Brown admitted.

"You go only now and then?"

"Once a year—the haberdashers' ball," Brown declared.

"You don't frequent—er—masquerades?"

"No; I think they're the limit. Why on earth do you ask me a fool question like that?"

"I was wondering whether you'd ever worn a red masquerade costume—a scarlet all-over gown."

"I'd look like a fool in anything like that," Brown said.

"Well, I needn't bother you any more just now," Haynes told him. "If you hear or see anything let me know, please."

"Surely. Only I'd hate to see a man go to the electric chair for killing Brayton."

Brown accompanied Detective Sam Haynes as far as the front door of the shop, and as the detective started away he heard the haberdasher giving orders to one of his clerks.

"Either innocent—or clever," was Haynes' comment.

CHAPTER XXII

CAUGHT IN A LIE

UNDER ordinary circumstances, Detective Sam Haynes was adept at reading men, but he was wise enough to know that a clever man who has committed a crime may exhibit great stupidity and give himself away, or a stupid man may become almost brilliant under stress and exhibit cleverness no man thought he possessed.

He had seen Brown long before, and had judged him to be an ordinary small business man who thought of nothing except increasing his trade, smoking a good cigar now and then, eventually marrying some nice home-loving girl and establishing himself in a small flat to grow old in peace.

Now, however, he found that Brown's attitude disconcerted him a bit; he did not know how to judge the man. At times Brown had seemed frightened; at other times it was almost as though he were having fun at the detective's expense.

But Haynes was in no hurry. He had decided to interrogate several suspects before he formed definite opinions regarding any one. His interview with Brown had netted him nothing except the sudden betrayal of interest on Brown's part when Haynes had asked him whether he frequented dances. Haynes could not guess what that meant; he had merely been leading up to the mention of a masquerade costume.

Now Haynes put thoughts of Brown out of his mind and turned into the main entrance of the building. He stopped at the cigar stand for a moment and purchased some cigars.

Then he saw Madame Violette's son, George Gray. From Rathway, Haynes had learned what had happened to Gray in relation to Brayton, how the boy had invested the money he had been handling for his mother, how Brayton had played upon the youth's ambition to be a financier. Gray was on the list of suspects, and Haynes stepped out from the cigar counter to stop and question him. He led the way around the side of the stairs, where there were a couple of chairs the janitor had neglected to carry into the basement. They sat down where they could talk without being overheard by anybody in the lobby. George Gray appeared half frightened; he seemed to be fighting to control fear. Haynes regarded him carefully as he spoke.

"You know what happened to Lorenzo Brayton, of course?"

"Yes."

"We are looking for his murderer," Haynes said. "So we are asking questions of everybody who knew him."

"I—I see."

"We are investigating every person who has had trouble with him in the recent past. It will be a very simple matter for every innocent person to clear himself."

"But why—why talk to me?" Gray asked.

"Didn't you have trouble with Brayton?"

"He robbed me. He lied to me and got me to invest my mother's money in one of his schemes, and it was nothing but a swindle! I told him it was, and he couldn't deny it. I had learned the facts."

"How?"

"I—I promised I'd not tell."

"But Brayton's murder changes all that," Haynes persisted. "Your promise won't hold now. And it shouldn't cause anybody annoyance, either. You'd better tell me, my boy."

"Satchley put me wise. He showed me the report a commercial agency had made. Satchley used to be Brayton's partner, but they split because Brayton was crooked."

"For your own information and for future reference, in case you should want to invest again, Satchley is every bit as crooked," Haynes told him. "Why did Satchley tell you about the swindle?"

"He didn't want me to lose my money."

"But you already had lost it."

"Then I—I don't know. He was just sore at Brayton, I guess, and wanted to cause him trouble."

"Do you suppose Satchley thought you'd take revenge on Brayton?"

"I don't know."

"Isn't it possible that Satchley didn't have courage himself, and hoped to set you on the man he hated?"

"He—he might have planned that," Gray said.

"What did you do when next you saw Brayton?"

"It—it was at home," the boy said, licking at his

dry lips and glancing around wildly. "I knew—and I was afraid to tell my mother. I was in my room, and Brayton and my mother were in the parlor. He —he was making love to her and——"

The boy stopped, and Haynes sensed the shame he felt at telling of his mother's foolishness.

"Go on," the detective said softly.

"He—he told her that the investment was all right, and that he would marry her as soon as the big deal was completed. I was just ready to jump into the other room and tell—because I knew that he was lying. It wasn't only about the investment—he was lying about marrying her. I knew he was just— just making love to her to get her money."

"Well?" Haynes asked, as the boy hesitated.

"But before I could get through the door, Madame Moonshine came in from the beauty parlor—I mean she came into the room where my mother and Brayton were. She had been listening—and a few hours before Brayton had promised to marry her—had talked to her just as he had been talking to mother."

"I understand."

"They cornered him, of course. He said that he had been unable to decide between them; but that they should not worry about their money, since it was all right. I knew better than that, so I sprang into the room and told him that he lied. I—I had a gun."

"You shot?"

"No. My mother stopped me just in time and took the gun away. Brayton left, and my mother sent me back into my room."

"See Brayton after that?"

"Almost every day," the boy admitted. "I—I— well, you can imagine how I felt. He had ruined us, and was unconcerned about it. You see, we couldn't touch him in court."

"I understand. Undoubtedly Brayton was a scoundrel. But we have to let the law deal with his murderer, for all that. Anything else to tell me?"

"About—what?"

"About you and Brayton," Haynes said. "You must realize that you are under suspicion to a certain extent."

"I didn't kill him."

"Where were you last night?"

"I didn't kill him, I tell you! I didn't!"

"Hush! Do you want to attract the attention of everybody in the lobby? If you didn't kill him, you can clear yourself easily enough, young man. You must be able to give me an alibi. Suppose that you begin with eight o'clock last night and tell me where you were between eight and midnight."

"Well," the boy replied, glancing away from Haynes and toward the entrance of the building, "I —I went to the cigar store down on the corner about eight, I think. I got some cigarettes, and I was talking to the clerk there for a few minutes."

"All right; that's the stuff. I can check up statements like that in a hurry and clear you of all suspicion," Haynes told him. "What else did you do?"

"I—I walked around a bit."

"Where?"

"No place in particular," the boy said. "I just

went up the street a few blocks, and dropped into a picture show."

"See anybody you knew there?"

"No. But I can tell you what the show was."

"Never mind that. You might have seen it during the afternoon; don't you understand? How long were you in the theater?"

"About an hour and a half, I guess."

"Then you left it about half past nine?"

"Or a quarter of ten."

"And then what did you do?" Haynes demanded. "Think well, now—and tell me everything, every little detail."

"I came back down the street toward home."

"Straight home?"

"No, sir. I didn't get home until almost midnight."

"Um! Where were you between a quarter to ten and midnight?"

The boy appeared to be more frightened now. He refused to meet the detective's eyes.

"I—I just walked around. It was hot, and I was worried about our business—didn't want to go to bed."

"Meet anybody you knew—talk to anybody?"

"Yes. I—I met George Brown."

"The haberdasher?"

"Yes, sir."

"What did you do?"

"We walked around for about a couple of hours—just walked around and talked. Brown was worried about business, too; Brayton had got his money."

"I know. What did you talk about?"

"N-nothing special."

Detective Sam Haynes was doing some rapid thinking. Brown had declared that he had seen nobody he knew, had talked to no one. Either Brown had lied, or else Gray was lying now.

"Come with me, Gray!" Haynes said suddenly.

"You—you mean to arrest me?"

"I am not arresting you. Just come with me. I want to prove your story."

"Oh!" The boy got up and walked at Haynes' side, and the detective led him straight into the establishment of Brown. The haberdasher was alone behind one of the counters.

"Brown," Haynes said, "I've been talking to this boy about the Brayton business. He seems to have a pretty good alibi. He says that between a quarter of ten and midnight he was walking around the streets with you, talking to you. That correct?"

Brown blinked his eyes rapidly.

"It is," he said finally.

"A short time ago you told me that you were pacing the pavements at that time, but that you neither saw nor talked to anybody you knew. How about it?"

"Isn't that peculiar?" Brown said. "I forgot all about George."

CHAPTER XXIII

TWO ARRESTS

BROWN'S smile disarmed Detective Sam Haynes for an instant. It seemed to be innocent, free of guile, yet Haynes felt that it was not. He stepped closer to the counter and spoke in a lower tone, not wishing anybody to overhear.

"Perhaps you have the idea that it is funny to treat an officer this way," Haynes said. "Let me give you a little thought for you to roll around in your mind for a few minutes. There are many detectives, good men, too, who would arrest you and young Gray this minute and have you locked up until you could tell the truth—the whole truth. You are in a bad position and do not realize it."

"Didn't mean to offend," Brown said.

"Do you realize that you are under suspicion in regard to the murder of Lorenzo Brayton? Do you know that a man found guilty of murder is likely to die in the electric chair?"

His last statement seemed to strike terror suddenly to the heart of George Gray. Madame Violette's son pressed close against the detective and looked up at him from bulging eyes set in a face dead-white.

"I didn't have anything to do with it," he gasped. "I told you the truth. I was walking around with Brown——"

"And Brown told me earlier in the day that he was walking by himself and did not see or speak to anybody he knew. How do I know that he isn't lying now to shield you? Or possibly he was lying in the first place to shield himself. Brown, you'd better talk. What were you and this boy so interested in that you had to discuss it for four hours on the street?"

"We were just companions in misery," Brown declared. "We were talking about the money we had lost, talking about the good luck other people have——"

"That's it!" the boy declared. "We just walked around and talked about things."

"Suppose the two of you do some hard thinking now. In all that time, did you two see anybody else you knew, talk to them?"

"I'm quite sure not," Brown declared.

"N-no—we didn't," the boy added.

"Then you have nothing to establish an alibi. It begins to look bad for you," Haynes declared.

"But such an idea is ridiculous," Brown declared. "If I had been going to shoot Lorenzo Brayton, I'd have fixed it so I would have had a dandy alibi. I'll bet there were five thousand men walking around the streets last night because of the heat who couldn't tell you to-day just where they had been, whom they had seen, and what they had said, if anything."

"Very plausible, and I do not doubt it," Haynes told him; "but I am interested only in you and George Gray at this moment. However, I'll consider the matter later. But after this, Brown, you'd better remember everything unless you want to get into trouble."

Brown excused himself suddenly and stepped to the other end of the counter. A middle-aged woman had entered from the street and was standing there. Haynes and George Gray were shielded from her sight by a show case packed with cravats.

"Good morning, Mrs. Murphy," they heard Brown say.

"I'd like a pair of number ten socks—plain black, and cheap," the woman replied. "They're for my man of all work. You know the kind he generally gets?"

Brown did. He got the socks and wrapped them up, and Mrs. Murphy handed him the exact change. Then she leaned across the counter, and though she spoke rapidly and in a low tone, and though Brown evidently was trying to signal her to be careful, she did not catch the signal. Detective Sam Haynes could make out her words easily.

"It's—terrible! What shall we do, Mr. Brown? Why didn't you stay at the house later last night? I told you when Mr. Raoul left at nine that you should remain until we knew for certain."

"But, Mrs. Murphy——" Brown began, his face flushing.

"And now—now I don't know what to think. This—this crime has shaken me. Oh, I pray, Mr. Brown, that everything will be all right—that we'll come out of it all right."

She dabbed at her eyes with a handkerchief and walked rapidly to the front door, while Brown began putting socks back in a box, trying to gain time and recover his composure.

Detective Sam Haynes' face had a determined look in it now. He grasped George Gray by the arm.

"Who was that woman?" he demanded.

"She—she's Mrs. Mary Murphy—runs a boarding house a couple of blocks down the street. My mother and I used to board with her until about a year ago."

"And so you were at her house last night between eight and twelve, were you? And you told me—— Just come with me, young man!"

Haynes grasped Gray more firmly and led him around the show case and up to the counter behind which Brown was standing.

"So you lied to me again!" he accused Brown. "You just told me that you and Gray didn't see anybody you knew between eight and twelve, and now this woman speaks of you being at her house, of Gray leaving about nine and of you remaining for a time longer. What have you to say for yourself, Brown?"

Brown's face had gone white now, and he was breathing rapidly. He looked Haynes straight in the eyes, and then out toward the street. Two or three times he seemed on the verge of speech but checked himself. Finally he gulped out the words:

"I—I haven't anything more to say just now, officer, except that I didn't kill Brayton."

"Naturally the murderer would say that," Haynes retorted. "And do you happen to know who did?"

Brown hesitated and looked uncomfortable. "No," he answered, after a time.

"It took you a long time to say it," Haynes declared. "So you were at Mrs. Murphy's house at nine, and this young man left about that time and you stayed on? Both of you seem to have a few hours to account for, it seems to me."

"I—I have nothing more to say," Brown gasped.

"Have *you?*" Haynes demanded, whirling upon George Gray suddenly.

"N-no, sir," the boy replied.

Detective Sam Hayes was just in time to catch a signal passing between them.

He glanced toward the lobby of the building and saw a uniformed officer there. Haynes beckoned, and the officer hurried inside.

"Take in these two men," Haynes ordered. "Suspected of murder in the first degree. Be quiet about it. They are to see nobody until I report. You understand?"

"I getcha!" the officer said.

There was the sudden clinking of handcuffs being withdrawn from the policeman's pocket.

"I—I——" George Gray began, in sudden fear.

"Shut up, you young fool!" Brown said.

The eyes of the two men met and seemed to clash, and then George Gray subsided and held out his hands, looking away as he did so, the tears starting from his eyes. Brown was cooler. He called to his head clerk:

"I've been pinched," he explained, "just because I saw fit not to talk my head off to an officer. Take charge of things until I get back, will you? Be sure that you have that new shipment of shirts unpacked this afternoon and put on display, and move that odd lot of socks if you can."

"Yes, sir."

"If I'm not back by to-morrow noon, pay the bills you'll find on the left end of my desk, and collect those on the right."

"Yes, sir."

"Have the front windows washed this afternoon, too. That boy has been growing lazy lately."

"I'll see to it, sir."

The clerk glared at Detective Sam Haynes and the policeman and retired. Brown whirled around and stepped from behind the counter. He, too, held out his wrists.

"Let's make the trip in a taxi," he said. "I'll pay the bill, if it is necessary."

CHAPTER XXIV

AS soon as Brown had been handcuffed, Haynes signed to the policeman to take his prisoners away, and then darted out of the door and began following Mary Murphy.

He caught sight of her almost immediately, for she had stopped at a grocery store a few doors down the street, and now was walking on toward her establishment. Haynes shadowed her from a short distance, watching closely to see whether she spoke to anybody.

But it appeared that Mrs. Murphy had completed her regular morning shopping tour. She waddled down the street and finally turned in at her own door. Haynes walked past the house to the corner, and then retraced his steps. He wanted to give Mrs. Murphy time to get settled at home before he interviewed her.

He walked up the steps and pulled at the bell. A girl answered his ring, and ushered him into a tiny parlor in the front of the house. Haynes waited no longer than two minutes before Mrs. Murphy entered the room and walked across to him. The look on her face was that of a landlady about to interview a possible boarder.

"I'm Detective Haynes, police department!"

Haynes made the statement bluntly. He was adept at reading human beings, and he judged that the best way to attack Mrs. Murphy. The landlady's face expressed surprise and a little fear, and then she motioned for Haynes to be seated again, and sat down on another chair not far from him.

"You wished to see me about something?" she asked.

"Yes. I suppose that you have heard of the murder of Lorenzo Brayton, the broker?"

"I read about it in the paper this morning," Mrs. Murphy replied. "I did not know the man personally, but I have heard him spoken of many times."

"May I ask by whom?"

"My friend, Madame Violette, knew him well and believed him to be a splendid gentleman until recently, when she discovered that he was a swindler. And one of my girl boarders works for Madame Violette and has acted as manicure for Mr. Brayton."

"I am investigating the crime," Haynes said. "We have several persons under suspicion, naturally —notably some who have had business trouble with Mr. Brayton. We seek to find where those persons were at the hour of the crime and so establish the innocence of those who are innocent."

"Oh, yes—I quite understand."

"So I'd like to ask you a few questions, principally about George Brown and Madame Violette's son, known as Raoul, whose real name is George Gray."

"I—I'll be glad to answer any questions I can."

"I am trying to establish where those two gentlemen were last night between eight and twelve o'clock.
I supposed you might know them and could help me."

"Indeed I know them. Both used to board with
me. And I think that I can help a little," Mrs.
Murphy replied. "Mr. Brown and George Gray
came to my house last night about a quarter of nine
o'clock."

"And how long did they remain?"

"George Gray went away in about fifteen or
twenty minutes."

"And Mr. Brown stayed on?"

"Mr. Brown remained about half an hour longer;
I think he left about nine thirty," Mrs. Murphy answered.

"Just a friendly call, then?"

"Y-yes, that was it."

"Please be frank with me, Mrs. Murphy," Detective Haynes said. "It will prove better for all concerned."

"I'm sure I don't know what you mean."

"You saw Mr. Brown this morning. I was standing a few feet away behind a show case and heard
your conversation with him. You were distraught
about something. You asked him why he didn't
stay at your house later last night—said he should
have stayed until he knew for certain! Knew what
for certain, Mrs. Murphy? And what did you mean
by telling him that you prayed everything would be
all right?"

Haynes bent forward as he asked the questions, his
eyes searching those of the landlady, watching her

carefully, watching every expression of her face, trying to understand the workings of her mind.

Plainly she was disconcerted for a moment. She looked puzzled, bewildered, a little afraid.

"I—I don't understand," she gasped.

"Just answer my questions, please. Why did Brown and Gray come here last night? What did you and Brown talk about after the boy left your house? And what did you mean by those statements to Brown in his store a short time ago?"

Mrs. Mary Murphy had regained her composure now. It was not difficult for her to do. She always had fought the world, and she had been running a New York boarding house for years; it took a great deal to disconcert her for more than an instant.

"That just goes to show," she replied, laughing a bit, "what importance can be attached to common language. I'll be glad to explain what I meant.

"One of my boarders is a young lady named Margaret Dranger. She came to us recently from Chicago. I knew her years ago; I worked for her father once, in fact. He formerly was in good circumstances, but he failed in business and the girl had to go to work. She came to me here, and I sent her to Madame Violette, where she got a job."

"Very well."

"She is an excellent girl—attractive and sensible both, something you don't find every day. Madame Violette assures me that she is a treasure. And she is an excellent stenographer as well as a manicure."

"Stenographer?"

"Yes; she worked for her father once, and then in

a railway office in Chicago. But she was tired of that work and wanted a beauty-parlor job instead. So she went to Madame Violette."

"But—about Brown?"

"I am coming to that," said Mrs. Murphy. "The afternoon before the haberdashers' annual ball, Mr. Brown went into Madame Violette's place to be manicured. Margaret waited on him, and he seemed to take an instant liking to her. They had a talk, and he asked her to go to the ball with him. She agreed."

"Well?"

"Mr. Brown fell in love with her instantly. He had been so busy building up his business that he had paid no attention to girls. It was quite a romance, and I wished to see it go through to the end. I know that Mr. Brown is a sensible, hard-working man sure to make his way in the world, and I loved Margaret and wanted to see her settled and happy."

"I understand."

"Then came this Brayton crash, and Mr. Brown lost all his money. He knew that he would have to start at the bottom again. I tried to tell him that it would make no difference to Margaret—wanted him to ask her to marry him. He was a bit timid about it. Yesterday evening, at closing time, he met her in the lobby of the building, took her into his office, and asked her."

"And what was her answer?" Haynes asked.

"He didn't get a definite answer. She told him that she admired him and would think it over. She said for him to call later in the evening for his answer."

"And he brought young Gray with him on such an occasion!"

"That was really funny. George Gray met him on the street and just hung onto him. So they came here together. But Margaret was not here, and soon Gray guessed there was something in the air and that Brown was waiting for the girl, so he left. Then Brown talked to me, and said that he was afraid Margaret would not take him because he had been such a fool as to let himself be swindled."

"Where was the girl?"

"She had gone out walking, to think it over. Brown waited here until about nine thirty, and then insisted upon going. He said that he was sure she would not take him, and was staying away until he had gone home, and he blamed it all on Brayton. He was most miserable."

"And that was what you meant by saying you wished he had waited until he was certain, and that you hoped it would be all right?"

"Yes, that is what I meant."

"And so he went away from here about nine thirty, cursing the name of Lorenzo Brayton?"

"I am afraid that he did. By the way, what time was Mr. Brayton killed?"

"A few minutes after ten o'clock," Haynes said, watching her closely. "So Brown could have done it, couldn't he?"

Mrs. Murphy's face went white instantly and she almost sprang from her chair.

"Then you have made me say something that may condemn him!" she cried. "Oh, he didn't do it! George Brown couldn't have done it!"

"That is to be determined," Haynes said gravely. "The story he told me to-day was full of holes. And George Gray's story was no better. Gray declared that he was with Brown until midnight, that they walked around the streets and talked."

"There is some terrible mistake!"

"Let us hope so, Mrs. Murphy. I'd a lot rather find out in the end that Brown didn't do it. And this Miss Dranger—do you think she means to marry Brown?"

"I do not know. I didn't get a chance to speak to her this morning. She got up late and had to hurry through her breakfast and go to work."

"How late did she remain out last night, Mrs. Murphy?"

"It was after eleven when she got in, but I don't think she met Mr. Brown."

"May I see her room?"

"Margaret's? Why?"

"I often can read a person's character by her home," Haynes said. "Possibly I can get an idea of what sort of influence she may have had on Brown. It might help to show that he wouldn't think of murder when there was a chance of winning such a girl."

"You just come with me," Mrs. Murphy said. "Margaret's room is the best kept in the house. She'd not be ashamed to have you see it."

A moment later he stood inside the room. It was, as the landlady had said, well kept. It had a cheerful appearance. The toilet articles on the dressing table were orderly. Nothing was scattered about the floor.

Haynes walked across it and turned to look it over carefully, while Mrs. Murphy remained at the hall door.

"That's her typewriter," the landlady said. "She brought it with her. Later she may do some stenographic work here at home and make extra money. She hopes to meet some business men at Madame Violette's and get their work."

Haynes lifted the cover of the typewriter.

"Seems to be a good machine," he said.

He bent lower and inspected it. An ordinary black ribbon was on the spools. Detective Sam Haynes rubbed the tips of two fingers over the keys, which were not newly cleaned. He glanced at his fingertips afterward and almost gasped. Again he bent over the machine and inspected it, paying special attention to the keys.

There could be no denying it—some of the letters were rimmed with red ink. Though there was a black ribbbon on the machine now, there had been a red ribbon used recently!

CHAPTER XXV

AWARE that Mrs. Murphy, Margaret Dranger's landlady, was watching him carefully, Detective Sam Haynes did not betray his sudden interest; but his mind was busy. Was there a better understanding between Margaret Dranger and Brown than Mrs. Murphy had intimated? Had Margaret Dranger written the cards in red for Brown, or George Gray? Had she written on her typewriter the letter to Brayton regarding The Scarlet Scourge?

Feeling that the landlady admired Margaret Dranger, Haynes did not want to intimate now that Miss Dranger had anything to do with the affair. He decided to see the girl and talk with her if possible before she learned the news of Brown's arrest.

There were other suspects on his list, too—Madame Moonshine and Madame Violette. Haynes did not intend to ignore any of them. There was a possibility that The Scarlet Scourge was an idea formulated by several persons; that more than one was involved. It might even be a wholesale attempt to settle the score with Lorenzo Brayton. Possibly there had been no intention of murdering at first, but somebody had been unable to withhold his hand when a chance was seen to make Brayton pay the great price.

Haynes pretended to be examining the room again for a time, and then he went back to the door.

"Your Miss Dranger seems to be a nice young woman," he told the landlady. "If she truly admires Brown, I hope, for her sake, that he will be proved innocent. I'm very much obliged to you, Mrs. Murphy."

He left the house and walked slowly down the street, going toward the office building again. There seemed to Haynes to be a hundred angles to this case; and he was beginning to be convinced that there was more than one person involved.

Just before he reached the entrance to the building, he came face to face with Rathway.

"Glad that I met you," Rathway said. "I wanted to talk to you, and didn't want to do it where other people might watch us. I understand that you arrested Brown and George Gray.

"I sent them in on suspicion," Haynes said. "They told stories with flaws in them, and since then I have discovered more flaws."

"Would you mind explaining to me?"

Haynes did so in as few words as possible. Rathway appeared to be very thoughtful.

"Pardon me if I say I think you may be on the wrong track," Rathway said when Haynes had concluded. "As you have said, Brown and the boy lied. But it may have been because of fear. They might not have been willing to tell what they were doing last night unless they believed it absolutely necessary. Perhaps they feared to throw suspicion on somebody else they liked."

"It is possible," Haynes admitted.

"I've got some information that may be of use to you—neglected to tell you before. It is about a girl named Margaret Dranger, who works for Madame Violette."

"What of her?" Haynes asked. "I understand that George Brown is eager to marry her."

"Is that so? It complicates matters. Perhaps both of us are on the right trail but working from opposite ends. Margaret Dranger is the stepdaughter of a man named Bethwell. Her mother died when she was young, and this Bethwell reared her. She thought a great deal of him. He ran a printing plant in Chicago. The girl studied stenography and worked for her stepfather in the office for a time, just to be near him."

"I understand," Haynes said.

"Lorenzo Brayton and Satchley—who was then his partner—got their hands on this Bethwell. The girl was away at school at the time. Bethwell finally had persuaded her that he was going to be rich and that she should be taught to be a lady. Brayton and Satchley stripped Bethwell clean, after their usual methods. Bethwell, realizing that even his business was gone and that he could never give Margaret the advantages he hoped to be able to give her, attempted suicide."

"Did he succeed?"

"No. But he injured himself so that he is an imbecile. He is in a sanitarium near Chicago, wrecked physically and mentally. The girl did all that she could for him, working at a job all the time. A short time ago she came here and went to Mrs. Murphy's boarding house. Years ago Mrs. Murphy cooked for her father. She sent Margaret to Madame Violette, and Madame Violette gave her a job. She didn't try for a position as stenographer, mind you— but went into the beauty parlor—in the building where Lorenzo Brayton had his office. Can you get the idea of a girl like that determining to have revenge on the men who robbed her stepfather and drove him insane? The Scarlet Scourge, remember, made Brayton write a check and then forced Satchley to cash it."

"Looks good," Haynes commented, thinking of the other information he had.

"She may not have done it herself, of course. If Brown was in love with her, and Brown had been stung by Brayton, too, possibly she got Brown to do it. And she is in it deeper than I have told you already, too."

"How is that?" Haynes asked.

"I've had my eye on Miss Margaret Dranger. I knew her story, thought she might be after Brayton, and believed she might put me on the right track to landing him for myself. The night before Brayton got that letter which was alleged to have been sent by Martin Cogblen, Margaret Dranger went to Newark. I followed her. She went to Newark and mailed two letters and a package, and came right back to New York again. Figure it out! Brayton got a letter and a package, and Satchley got a letter —all from Newark. Those letters made it possible for The Scarlet Scourge to catch Brayton and Satchley in their offices at a late hour at night."

"Looks good," Detective Sam Haynes commented again. "You certainly are a help, Rathway."

"But I mustn't appear in this, remember. Nothing is to be said even to the men in my own department. Your chief promised."

"Don't worry about that, Rathway."

"I'd get mine from Washington if it leaked out. We are after others of Brayton's ilk, and if it became known they'd cover their tracks, as they have done before. I'll see you later, Haynes, and may have more information."

Rathway went on down the street, and Detective Sam Haynes hurried toward the modiste establishment of Madame Moonshine. Because evidence was commencing to point to Margaret Dranger and George Brown, it did not follow that Haynes would neglect other suspects. And Madame Moonshine certainly was a suspect. Brayton had trifled with her affections and had swindled her into the bargain. And Madame Moonshine was the sort of woman likely to go after such a man with a gun held ready for use.

Madame Moonshine was in her establishment. Haynes made himself known and requested a private interview, and the modiste took him into her office. The detective made an instant effort to visualize her character from her appearance. She was a good-looking woman, and had once been a beauty. Haynes judged that she was proud and romantic, and that she had a latent temper that was ready to burst into storm at the slightest provocation.

She turned a bit white when Haynes mentioned

Brayton s violent death, and then her eyes narrowed and she tapped her desk nervously with the tips of her fingers as she watched him.

"Have you information of any sort that you feel might help me?" the detective asked. "I grant you that Brayton was a scoundrel, but murder is murder even when a scoundrel is the victim."

Madame Moonshine appeared to be thinking deeply.

"You suffered a loss through Brayton, didn't you?" Haynes asked.

"He swindled me out of several thousand dollars," Madame Moonshine admitted, a hard look coming into her face.

"Did he lead you to believe that you were the object of his affections?"

"I may as well confess it," she replied, her face flushing. "I was a foolish woman. It was his game to make women think he was in love with them, and thus get them to invest money in his worthless schemes. He did the same with Madame Violette. I think, since I am a business woman and supposed to have business sense, that I might have forgiven him the swindle—but I never could forgive the fact that he played with my heart."

Madame Moonshine's face assumed an expression that seemed to say Romance was dead so far as she was concerned, but Haynes remembered that this was a clever woman before him.

"Persons who have had trouble with Brayton are under suspicion, of course," he said. "We are eliminating these as quickly as possible. I'd like to have you give me an alibi—tell me where you were last night and what you were doing."

"At what time?" Madame Moonshine asked.

"Begin at eight o'clock, please."

"At eight o'clock I was in this very office, going over my books and wondering how to make payments as small as possible and still maintain my credit. I was writing out some orders, too."

"How late did you remain in the office, please?"

"It must have been a few minutes after nine when I left," Madame Moonshine replied.

"You went—where?"

"Home. I live in a small apartment a few blocks down the street. I'll give you the address, if you wish it."

She gave it, and Haynes made a note of it in a memorandum book.

"And you remained there the remainder of the evening?" he asked.

"I remained there all night, until I left to come to the shop this morning," Madame Moonshine answered.

Haynes could think of nothing more to ask. Madame Moonshine looked like a woman speaking the truth, and he knew that he could ascertain easily whether she had uttered a falsehood. He thanked her and took his leave, and went through the lobby and up the stairs toward the beauty parlor of Madame Violette.

When he entered nobody was in the front room except the cashier and Margaret Dranger. Haynes asked for Madame Violette, and the cashier called her. The detective stepped to one side and spoke in a low voice. He gave her his identity and asked for a private conversation.

A moment later Haynes found himself in the little parlor of Madame Violette's living apartment. Madame Violette, Haynes knew at a glance, was not French. In fact, he knew that the name was assumed for business reasons. Madame Violette appeared to have been laboring under strong emotion, too.

"I wish to speak to you in regard to the death of Lorenzo Brayton," Haynes began.

"But I know nothing about it."

"I am interviewing those who knew the man, those with whom he had business dealings," Haynes told her. "You may have some information that will be of great aid to me. I understand that he handled some money for you."

"He stole my savings!" Madame Violette declared in a harsh voice. "And he persuaded my son to invest all our business money in a fake scheme. He ruined us, in fact."

"I suppose that you feel very bitter toward him?"

"Naturally."

"Did you ever wish his death?"

Madame Violette looked startled for a moment. "Possibly I did at first," she replied. "It is quite a blow to learn that a man you have trusted has robbed you."

"And there was some personal interest, was there not?"

"I am ashamed to admit it. I thought that the man cared for me. He made me care for him."

"Was your son very angry at Brayton?"

"He tried to shoot him, in this very room, as soon as we learned of the swindle. But I prevented that, and my son's anger cooled."

"Where was your son last night?"

Madame Violette looked at him, wild-eyed. "Surely you do not think that he committed that crime?"

"I am checking up on everybody who had a reason to hate Lorenzo Brayton," Haynes explained. "The easiest way to avoid suspicion is to prove innocence. A perfect alibi is the best proof."

"I know that my boy never did it—but I do not know where he was last night."

"What time did he leave home?"

"A few minutes before eight, I think."

"And he returned?"

"About midnight."

"Did you see him when he came in?"

"Yes. I was putting labels on some toilet lotion I sell."

"How did he look and act?" Haynes asked.

"Naturally. He talked to me for a few minutes, and then we both went to bed."

"And he didn't say where he had been?"

"No; and I didn't ask him," Madame Violette said. "I suppose that he had been bowling or playing pool. He does both now and then. It is the poor boy's only recreation except a baseball game once in two weeks."

"Well, we can drop the boy for the time being,"

Haynes told her. "Will you kindly tell me how you spent the evening?"

"I never left the place," Madame Violette said. "I was putting labels on bottles all evening."

"You were alone?"

"Not all the time. Madame Moonshine, the modiste on the ground floor, was here a part of the time."

"About what time, please?"

"She came in about nine o'clock and remained here until about ten."

Haynes looked thoughtfully out of the window at the busy street below. Madame Moonshine had declared that she had gone home about nine o'clock and had remained there. Either Madame Moonshine had lied, or else Madame Violette was lying now. It was a thing to be determined later.

"Madame Moonshine went home at ten?" he asked.

"She said that she was going right home."

Haynes sat up straighter in his chair.

"Madame Violette," he said, "please call Miss Margaret Dranger, who works for you. I want to ask her a few questions."

CHAPTER XXVI

A STERN EXAMINATION

MARGARET came into the room slowly, turning and closing the door after her entrance, and then stepped across to a chair placed in about the middle of the room. There was a questioning look in her face, and something more. Detective Sam Haynes could not decide whether it was a look of fear or merely wonder that she had been called to this conference.

She sat down in the chair Madame Violette indicated, and looked first at her employer and then at Haynes, as though to ask what they required of her.

"This gentleman is a detective," Madame Violette said. "He is investigating the murder of Lorenzo Brayton, and wishes to ask you a few questions, I believe. He has asked me some. I imagine everybody in the building is being interrogated. There is nothing to fear, my dear girl, so do not get nervous. Just tell him what he wishes to know, if you can."

Madame Violette sat down, and Margaret looked across at Haynes once more.

"I am ready," she said simply. "What is it that you wish to ask me?"

"Did you know Brayton?"

"By sight. I manicured him once or twice."

"Never saw him before you came to work here?"

"No, sir."

"Ever hear of him before?"

"Yes, sir. The very day I came here Madame Violette said that a Mr. Brayton was one of her particular customers, and that if I manicured him I was to be careful of his sore thumb."

"Um!" Haynes grunted. He was not sure whether the girl was making fun of him. "You came from Chicago, didn't you?"

"Yes, sir."

"Ever hear of Brayton there?"

"Not by that name."

"What do you mean by that?" Haynes asked.

"In Chicago he went by the name of Tampley. He and Mr. Satchley swindled my father out of all his money."

"Why, Margaret, you never told me that!" Madame Violette exclaimed.

"I didn't know you'd be interested, madame." She faced Haynes again. "That is why I am working," she went on to say. "The swindle resulted in my father being sent to an insane asylum. He was my stepfather, really. His name was Bethwell."

"Why did you come to New York?"

"I had been in good circumstances in Chicago, and after my father was sent to the sanitarium I disliked to remain there. I had to go to work, you see, and there I knew so many persons in good circumstances that——"

"Just a little pride?"

"I suppose so," Margaret admitted. "And I

knew Mrs. Murphy here. She was our cook years ago. I got her address and wrote to her, and she said for me to come on. She recommended me to Madame Violette, and madame was kind enough to give me a place here."

"You had no idea of following Brayton here and squaring accounts with him?"

"I may have wished that I could do so. But I am only a girl."

"Have you liked it here?"

"Every one has been so kind."

"You've had a little romance, haven't you?"

"Sir?"

"I do not wish to pry into your personal affairs, but it is necessary just now. Mr. Brown, the haberdasher, has been very attentive, has he not?"

"He has been very kind. I went to a dance with him and have gone walking with him several times since."

"Are you engaged to him?" Haynes asked.

"No, sir. I scarcely could be, since he never asked me to be his wife."

"Didn't he ask you last evening as you started home from work?"

"Why, no, sir!"

"And didn't you tell him that you'd think it over, and for him to call later for his answer?"

"No, sir. I never heard of such a thing. Mr. Brown has been attentive—and I like him—and maybe I dreamed he might ask me such a question. But he has not. I suppose it is because he lost money to Mr. Brayton."

Haynes frowned and looked out of the window again. So Mrs. Murphy had lied to him—or else this girl was lying now. Mrs. Murphy had concocted an interesting romance, it appeared, that did not have any foundation in fact.

"Do you go to many dances?" Haynes asked.

"No, sir. I've been to but the one since I came here—the evening with Mr. Brown."

"You don't go in for masquerades?"

"I never attended one in my life. I think they are silly."

"Then I suppose you haven't a collection of masquerade costumes or anything like that. Do you like red as a color?"

"Not particularly. What a silly question!"

"Scarlet?" Haynes persisted.

"That—that is a shade of red, really, isn't it?" she asked. Haynes imagined that she was disconcerted for an instant.

"Did you ever work except as a manicure?"

"Yes, as a stenographer. I was my stepfather's stenographer for a time."

"Um! Got a machine?"

"Yes, sir—in my room. I keep in practice, you see."

Haynes saw that the girl was either innocent or very clever. She made no effort to hide anything. Suddenly he took from his pocket one of the cards The Scarlet Scourge had left in Satchley's office, and handed it to her.

"Know what make of machine that was written on?" he demanded, in a louder tone.

She looked him straight in the eyes and then examined the card.

"I—I couldn't say," she said. "You will find that sort of type on several makes of typewriters."

"Ever use a red ribbon on your machine?"

"In my father's office, when I was writing loose leaves to go into his account books."

"How long ago was that?"

"Two years ago," she said. "I haven't done any work as stenographer or typist since—since father went insane."

"I suppose you keep your machine in repair—and cleaned?"

"Of course! I'd be a poor typist if I did not—and typewriters are expensive."

Detective Sam Haynes bent toward her suddenly.

"Miss Dranger," he said, "I saw your typewriter a short time ago. There is red ink on the keys."

"I—I beg your pardon?"

"And it hasn't been there for two years. Moreover, I glanced at the number of the typewriter. I know something about typewriters. And I know that that particular machine was not made two years ago."

"Oh, I didn't say this was the same machine I used in father's office. It isn't. That machine was sold with the other things when father was swindled. My present machine I bought about a year ago when I thought that I'd do some private work to make money."

"But the red ink on the keys?"

"Why—why—I scarcely can believe that. I don't

see how it could be. But I haven't used the machine for several days."

"Um!" Haynes grunted again. "How did you spend your time last night?"

"I went home from work and ate supper, and then went to my room."

"Remain there?"

"No, sir," she said frankly. "I left about eight o'clock."

"May I ask where you went?"

"I walked around for a time, and finally went to the motion picture show on the avenue."

"When did you leave there?"

"It must have been after ten o'clock—it was quite a long show. I am sure it was after ten o'clock?"

"See anybody you knew?"

"No, sir."

"Neither at the show nor on the street?"

"Neither," she said.

"Go straight home after you left the picture theater?"

"No, I didn't," she confessed. "It was warm, and I felt that I wanted to walk. So I—I walked."

"What time did you get home?"

"I am afraid it was almost midnight."

So she was making no effort to lie there! Detective Sam Haynes was a bit puzzled. Surely she must see what he was driving at with his questions.

"Do you mean to tell me that you walked around the streets for almost two hours?"

"Yes, sir."

"At that time of night!"

Margaret Dranger's face flushed. "I don't think you have the right to take that tone to me," she said. "I walked up the avenue for quite a distance, and came back. I have had a great deal of trouble," she went on in explanation. "I was thinking of father. I—I wanted to think of him. And I was afraid that, if I went back home, some of the other boarders would want to talk or sing or play cards. I didn't feel like doing any of those things."

"I understand. Have you ever heard Mr. Brown threaten to harm Brayton?"

"No, sir."

"Ever hear anybody else threaten?"

"No, sir."

"Did you ever see that card printed in red before?"

"You—you are making me nervous with your questions," she said.

"Answer me!"

"N-no, sir."

"So you just walked up and down the avenue from ten o'clock until midnight?"

"Just as I told you, sir."

"And didn't see or talk to anybody you knew?"

"No, sir."

"You had reasons to hate Brayton," Haynes said. "He was shot between ten and eleven o'clock."

The girl looked at him, wild-eyed.

"You—you mean that you think I did it?" she asked. "Oh, I didn't! I couldn't shoot anybody! I couldn't even kill a little bird! I'd never—never do such a thing!"

"Take it quietly," Haynes advised. "I never said that you killed him. I'm merely trying to find out who did."

The girl appeared on the verge of hysterics now.

"We'll say no more about it at present, Miss Dranger," Haynes said soothingly. "You must understand that I am only doing my duty."

"I—I understand that, sir. May I go now, please?"

"Yes, you may go."

Margaret got slowly out of the chair and turned toward the door. Haynes was watching her closely, and Madame Violette was making little sounds of pity deep down in her throat. But before the girl could reach the door, it was opened, and Madame Moonshine came bouncing into the room.

She stopped quickly and in confusion when she saw Haynes sitting by the window. Margaret Dranger brushed past her and went into the beauty parlor, and the door was closed.

"I—I just ran in to see you——" Madame Moonshine began, glancing at Madame Violette.

"This gentleman is——" Madame Violette began.

"I already have met Madame Moonshine," Haynes interrupted. "I was asking her some questions before I came here. And I'd like to ask you one more, Madame Moonshine."

"What is it, sir?"

"You said that you left your shop last night and went right home. Madame Violette tells me that you were up here until quite a late hour. She says that you came here about nine o'clock and left at ten. I want to ask you, Madame Moonshine, why you told me an untruth."

There was silence for a moment. Madame Moonshine's face presented a multitude of changes in an instant. Then she threw back her head and laughed lightly.

"I—I beg your pardon," she said. "I'm quite sure I forgot all about it. Of course I was here between nine and ten. I didn't mean an untruth, I assure you."

"You were very forgetful," Haynes said, not without some sarcasm. "Now would you mind telling me, if you left here at ten o'clock, where you went?"

"I went straight home," Madame Moonshine declared. "I just visited with Madame Violette a while."

"You are forgetting nothing this time?"

"I am quite sure not," Madame Moonshine said.

The door from the beauty parlor was thrown open again, and the little cashier rushed in and up to Madame Violette.

"Oh, madame, madame!" she cried. "Your son has been arrested for murdering Mr. Brayton— your son and Mr. Brown!"

CHAPTER XXVII

THE SCARLET ROBE

"EVERYBODY is a liar," Detective Sam Haynes told himself. "What a cinch a detective would have if everybody told the truth!"

He had left the beauty parlor and now came to the head of the stairs, having determined to walk down the one flight instead of waiting for the elevator. Halfway down the stairs he glanced over the side, down to where he and George Gray had had their talk earlier in the day. Then he drew back his head quickly. Directly beneath him was Margaret Dranger, without hat or coat on, just as she had hurried from the beauty parlor. She was talking to old Frand, the janitor.

Haynes could scarcely hear the words.

"Don't you tell a soul, Mr. Frand," the girl was saying. "It might cause trouble, you know."

"I'll not say a single word, miss," Frand replied.

"Be careful. You might tell when you're not thinking."

"You can trust me, miss."

Haynes glanced over the side of the stairs again. Margaret Dranger was leaving the janitor, and in a moment she would be coming up the steps. Haynes walked out to the middle and began to descend.

They met not far from the bottom, and Haynes

lifted his hat politely. The girl nodded to him and hurried on, her face white and drawn. Haynes went down leisurely, made sure that Margaret had gone on to the beauty parlor, then turned back toward the door that opened into the basement and janitors' quarters.

"I want to speak to you, Frand," he said.

"What is it, sir?"

"I just overheard your conversation with the young woman who works for Madame Violette. She told you not to tell something that you knew, that it might cause trouble if you did. I want to know what it is, Frand."

"But I—I promised her that I'd not tell," the old janitor protested.

"I know that you did, Frand. But I am insisting, as an officer of the law, that you tell me."

"I—I don't want to get anybody into trouble, sir," Frand said.

"But there has been a murder committed, Frand. Now I want to know everything that goes on in this building."

"It—it wasn't anything much," Frand said.

"Tell me!" Haynes commanded.

Frand looked down the hall toward the lobby, and his face flushed slowly.

"I—I can't tell you," he said.

"Want to go to jail?" Haynes asked quickly, in a stern voice.

"That—that would kill me, sir. I've had about all I can endure lately."

"What?"

"The—the loss of my money, sir, for one thing. Brayton swindled me. It was all I had for my old age, and now I don't know what will become of me when I can work no longer. And that won't be long now. I'm getting old and weak."

"What was the young woman talking to you about, Frand? It may save a lot of trouble if you tell me."

"I don't like to tell, sir."

"It's the best thing for you to do, Frand. Nobody can blame you for it, because an officer compels you to speak."

Frand hesitated a moment, and then looked up at Haynes squarely.

"I am sure that it doesn't amount to anything, sir," he said. "It—it was just a funny dress that I found."

"Dress?"

"A funny red dress, sir."

"I want to see it," Haynes said, his heart hammering at his ribs despite his experience in unraveling murder mysteries.

Frand led the way down to the janitors' room and got it from his locker. He spread it out on the table, and Haynes inspected it quickly. It was a long, voluminous scarlet robe, with a hood attached. Inside the hood was a scarlet mask. Scarlet gloves of the same material were in a pocket of the robe.

"The Scarlet Scourge!" Haynes gasped. "Frand, this is very important. Tell me where you found it, and when—and do not forget a single thing."

"It was after the—the murder, sir. You officers were running around the place and causing a lot of excitement. It was about midnight or a little later last night, sir. I was going along the hall-way on the second floor, sir, and I found the funny dress in the hall."

"Where?" Haynes demanded.

"Right near the door to Madame Violette's beauty parlor, sir. It was all rolled up, and had been tossed there, I guess. This morning about ten o'clock, just before I went off duty, I asked the young lady about it. I went to Madame Violette's, thinking one of her girls had lost the dress, but nobody was in the front room except the young lady. She—she told me to keep it down here until she found out, sir. And just a few minutes ago she came down and told me to be sure and not mention to anybody that I had found the dress. I suppose, sir, that maybe one of the young women has been getting into some sort of a scrape."

"Possibly that is it," Haynes said. "I'm going to take the dress for a time, Frand. Wrap it in a piece of newspaper. Don't tell anybody that I mentioned the affair to you. You'll get in trouble with the police if you do."

"I'll do just as you say, sir," Frand replied. He rolled the dress in a piece of newspaper, and Haynes took it and departed.

He was thinking swiftly as he ascended to the ground floor. So Margaret Dranger had been afraid that he would find out about the scarlet robe! And why had she not taken it from Frand herself? Because she was afraid it would be found in her possession?

Haynes intended at first to await developments, but as he came to the bottom of the stairs he changed his mind and hurried up them. He entered the beauty parlor again. Madame Violette was in her own room in hysterics because of her son's arrest. Nobody was in the front room of the establishment except Margaret Dranger.

"One moment, Miss Dranger," Haynes said. He put the bundle on the table before her and began unwrapping it, watching her face closely meanwhile. He saw her start as she caught a glimpse of the scarlet.

"What Frand found in the hall just outside the door of the beauty parlor," Haynes said. "A few minutes ago you asked him not to mention to anybody that he had found it. Why?"

Haynes snapped the question at her. She seemed bothered for a moment, and then looked up at him frankly.

"I—I'm sorry Frand told you."

"I overheard you speaking to him, and forced him to tell. What about it?"

"I—I read about The Scarlet Scourge in the morning paper," she said, "and all about the murder. When Frand told me about finding the scarlet robe, I—I was afraid——"

"Afraid of what?"

"I—I was afraid that Madame Violette's son had dropped it," she said.

"You think he was The Scarlet Scourge—that he murdered Lorenzo Brayton?"

"No—no! But I knew he was almost insane because Mr. Brayton had swindled him, and for a moment I thought that possibly he had done it. Then, when I heard that he had been arrested, I thought it would look bad for him if you knew where the robe had been found. I don't think he did it—but I was afraid it would be—what you call damaging evidence. Madame Violette had been so kind to me that——"

Margaret Dranger began weeping softly, and felt for her handkerchief. Detective Sam Haynes started to wrap up the scarlet robe again.

"I understand," he said. "You have done your best; you are loyal to Madame Violette and her son. I'll not bother you any more at present."

He left the beauty parlor abruptly and went down the stairs again, and continued through the lobby. At the entrance of the building he met Peter Satchley face to face.

"I've been wondering whether I'd see you," Satchley said. "Got any trace of my ten thousand yet?"

"Not a trace," Haynes replied. "I'm looking for a murderer more than for your ten thousand dollars."

"Well, for Heaven's sake, shake somebody down and get the coin back!" Satchley said. "I can't afford to stand such a loss. Any developments?"

"Plenty of them, but nothing definite."

"You might as well pull off the man you have watching me," said Satchley. "Oh, I'm wise to him! He couldn't shadow a child. Pull him off. I didn't kill Brayton, and I didn't rob myself!"

Satchley went on toward the elevator, and Haynes stepped into the street and started toward the nearest subway station. Rathway came up from behind and touched him on the arm.

"I was waiting for you to leave the building," he said. "Anything new?"

"A lot," Haynes replied.

"Give us the news."

As they walked along, Haynes spoke in a low voice and rapidly, telling Rathway the results of his interviews.

"Cinch!" Rathway announced, when Haynes had concluded.

"What do you think?"

"I think that The Scarlet Scourge killed Brayton, of course. And either that Dranger girl is The Scarlet Scourge, or she knows who is. I'm inclined to think that Brown and Madame Violette's son are both infatuated with her, and that she got them to do away with Brayton. She was after Brayton herself—wanted revenge because of her father. When she learned that he had swindled Brown and the boy she joined forces with them. Either she fired the shot, or one of those men did at her instigation."

"There may be a great deal in what you say," Haynes replied. "I'm going to give both men the third degree. Possibly I'll see you to-morrow, Rathway."

Haynes hurried on toward the subway station. Rathway stood still, looking after him, a peculiar expression on his face. An observer would have said that Rathway believed Sam Haynes was not the best detective in the world.

CHAPTER XXVIII

PERHAPS Sam Haynes was not the best detective in the world, but he was an excellent one, nevertheless. His detective work was done from the standpoint of common sense only. He gathered information, digested it, arrived at a conclusion, and acted upon it.

Haynes went to headquarters, put the scarlet robe in his locker, had men assigned to watch over his several suspects, and then hurried to the detention jail to hold interviews with Brown and Madame Violette's son.

He asked a multitude of questions, seeing the men one at a time at first, and then confronting them together and showing them the flaws in their stories. Here and there he got a sentence that astonished him and gave him food for thought, but he reached a point where his prisoners absolutely refused to reply to another question, and so found himself up against a stone wall of stubbornness.

Then Detective Sam Haynes went back to the office building and into the suite where the tragedy had occurred. Locking the corridor door behind him, he conducted an exhaustive investigation again. He stood in the door between the two rooms, stood in the corridor door of the private office, examined every inch of the walls, the floor, the ceiling, looked at the filing cases and safe and other furniture.

He discovered several things of minor interest and one of importance. He sat down at Brayton's desk and reached for the telephone, and he conducted conversations with the medical examiner's office, and with the undertaking establishment that had Brayton's body.

Then Detective Sam Haynes left the office and went to the two rooms that constituted his bachelor home. He removed his shoes and put on his slippers, took off his collar and opened his shirt at the throat, filled and lighted a gigantic pipe, and sat in an easy-chair looking out at the street—and seeing nothing in it.

The pipe went out. Haynes filled and lighted it again. He was considering the evidence in hand, and applying his common sense to the situation.

One by one he considered his suspects, and then he viewed the entire situation from the outside, so to speak. Who was The Scarlet Scourge? That was his first question. Who had the motive and the opportunity both?

He dismissed the idea of Peter Satchley. He believed that Satchley had told the truth about the visit of The Scarlet Scourge, and he was convinced that Satchley, determined to square accounts with Lorenzo Brayton, would not have gone about it in such a childish manner. Satchley had expressed his true character when he had said that he would have hit Brayton in the purse, but would not have shot him in the back.

Brown had had an opportunity and a motive. He could have gone to Brayton's office immediately after leaving Mrs. Murphy's house.

George Gray would not give an account of his actions between the time he had left the Murphy house and midnight. He had had an opportunity and a motive.

Madame Moonshine might have dressed in the scarlet robe and committed the crime after leaving Madame Violette's. Madame Violette could have done it immediately after Madame Moonshine had left.

Margaret Dranger could have done it, of course, since she was absent, "walking around," at the hour. Frand, the janitor, could have done it and reached his elevator before Satchley escaped from the closet.

Two or more of them might have combined and done it!

The finding of the scarlet robe near the door of Madame Violette's beauty parlor did not point the way to the assassin, according to Haynes' manner of reasoning. The criminal, making his escape down the rear stairs of the building, would have dropped it there before going down the last flight to the street, or getting out of the second-story window to the roof of the small building adjoining. It would have been the logical place to drop it.

Haynes considered again all that the several suspects had told him. He digested the information given him by Rathway. Then he did some telephoning from his rooms, long-distance telephoning that promised a heavy bill at the end of the month that the city would have to pay.

One of these telephone conversations appeared to give him much food for thought. He got up and paced the floor of the room, his head hanging, the pipe out and clenched between his teeth in one corner of his mouth. He had considered the affair from the standpoint of common sense, and now he allowed himself to dream a bit.

Presently he grinned and began humming a tune. Once more he filled his pipe, and again he sat before the window, a smile on his lips. It was as though Detective Sam Haynes had solved some important problem and was greatly relieved.

"The Scarlet Scourge!" he murmured. "Um! Common sense does it every time. Bet a thousand to a cent I'm right! Why didn't I think of it in the first place? Chump!"

Haynes put on his shoes and his collar, after shaving and bathing his face in cold water, and went out upon the street again. His appearance was not that of a man who had gone without sleep and had been working hard on a murder case. He journeyed to a restaurant he liked, and ate a good meal in a manner that told those near him he had nothing on his mind. As a matter of fact, he had many things on his mind.

Then he drifted around the streets until dark, speaking to an acquaintance now and then, dropping into places where he was known—just spending the time.

Detective Sam Haynes intended making an experiment that night, and if it resulted as he hoped, his work would be done. If it did not, he would have to follow another line of reasoning.

Presently Haynes stepped into a drug store and went into a telephone booth. He called Rathway, who lived in a second-rate hotel not far away. Rathway happened to be in his room.

"This is Haynes," the detective said. "I've got a line on something very important, Rathway—something new. Maybe it will concern you as much as me."

"In regard to—er——" Rathway hesitated.

"Yes. It isn't only that particular case you told me, but you are working along lines that lead to other men and——"

"I understand."

"I wish you'd go to Columbus Circle about ten thirty to-night. Be on the south side of it and watch for me. It is very important. I haven't time to talk to you now—don't care to say too much over the telephone, anyway. Be there at ten thirty, and remain there until I show up. If I am not there by midnight, call it off. Maybe I'll not be able to make it."

"I understand. I'll do it, Haynes."

"If I shouldn't see you to-night, watch for me in the morning near the office building."

"All right."

Detective Sam Haynes, humming a bit of a song, went out upon the street again and turned northward. He took a cigar from his pocket, bit off the end of it, struck a match and lighted it, and puffed a cloud of fragrant smoke upward. He felt that he could really enjoy a smoke now.

He glanced at his watch and saw that it was almost ten o'clock. On up the street he went, hoping that Morton Rathway would reach the Circle and remain there for a time.

Rathway did manage to reach the Circle at about twenty-five minutes of eleven. He walked back and forth, watching the crowds, puffing at his cigarette, wishing that Detective Sam Haynes would put in an appearance and explain his peculiar telephone message.

At eleven o'clock he began to find the waiting monotonous. At eleven thirty Rathway confided to himself that it was a nuisance, and that something must have happened to delay Haynes.

At midnight, Morton Rathway was still waiting.

CHAPTER XXIX

A MESSAGE

NOR did Morton Rathway see Detective Sam Haynes that night or at any time the day following, but late in the afternoon he received a message from him, a letter delivered by a uniformed officer, and, as a result at eight o'clock that night Rathway was in the suite that had been used by Brayton.

There were several people in the suite. Brown and George Gray had been taken there from the detention jail, officers guarding them. Madame Violette was there, traces of tears on her face, sitting beside her son, with an arm around his shoulders protectingly. Madame Moonshine sat on the other side of the boy.

Margaret Dranger was there, because Sam Haynes had commanded her presence, and Mrs. Mary Murphy was with her. Margaret was glancing at Brown repeatedly. Her looks gave him courage; nevertheless, the haberdasher appeared ill at ease.

Frand, the old janitor, was there, for Haynes considered him an important witness. Peter Satchley sat in a chair tilted back against one of the walls.

"We hope to clear up the Brayton murder here and now," Detective Haynes said, after the door had been locked and an officer stationed in the corridor to keep away any curious person who might appear. "All you people in this room are interested more or less. Some of you have been under suspicion. Most of you have had trouble with Lorenzo Brayton. I am eager to settle this thing to-night, have the guilty person taken into custody, and relieve the minds of the innocent. I believe that the person who murdered Lorenzo Brayton is in this room now!"

A chorus of gasps answered the statement, and Haynes watched them looking at one another, trying to read their thoughts. Madame Violette pressed her son closer to her side and Margaret Dranger glanced at the haberdasher again.

"Some person called The Scarlet Scourge wrote letters purporting to have come from a man in Newark. Those letters made it necessary for Brayton and Mr. Satchley to be in their offices at a late hour at night. That person also mailed an electric battery to Brayton.

"On the night of the crime, shortly after the hour of ten, this Scarlet Scourge appeared in this office, went into Brayton's private office, and held Brayton up. The Scarlet Scourge did not speak, but used printed cards with which to convey commands. Brayton, it appears, was forced to write a check for ten thousand dollars payable to The Scarlet Scourge. Afterward this Scarlet Scourge forced Mr. Satchley to cash the check. I am merely stating facts, and do not intend to go into minor details, since the majority of you are familiar with them already.

"Later Mr. Brayton was found dead, shot, sitting in his desk chair and sprawled over his desk."

Haynes opened the door of the private office, in which the lights were burning.

"The chair was as you can see it now," he said. "The dead man was in it. The battery was there, and the papers in which it had been wrapped. Clear, isn't it? Brayton cried out for help, and The Scarlet Scourge, let us say, fearful of discovery, silenced him forever. Mr. Satchley, locked in the closet in his office, heard those cries soon after The Scarlet Scourge left him, and says that they stopped suddenly.

"Ladies and gentlemen, it must be clear to you. We want to find the one who impersonated The Scarlet Scourge!

"There is not a person in this room who could not have been The Scarlet Scourge! Mr. Satchley, who underwent the experience, declares that he could not tell whether it was man or woman, fat or thin, blond or brunet. The red robe was voluminous, the face and hand were covered, no word was spoken. That red robe was found later in the hallway near the door of Madame Violette's beauty shop.

"Who would impersonate such a character and force Brayton to write a check and Satchley to cash it? Who would be in a state of mind to wish Brayton's violent death? Almost all of you.

"I'll take Brown first. Brayton had stolen Brown's savings. Brown had a motive, one of the strongest in the world, that of revenge. Brown left

Mrs. Murphy's place on the night of the murder at nine thirty o'clock, and could have come right to this building and committed the crime. And Brown lied to me when I questioned him."

"I—I——" Brown began.

"Brown declared that he had walked around the streets all evening and had met nobody he knew. I ascertained afterward that he was with George Gray for some time, and also paid a visit to Mrs. Murphy's house. That visit had an element of mystery about it, too."

"I—I'll talk!" Brown said suddenly. "I never killed Brayton. But I was about ready to do it! You can't blame me; he robbed me of all my savings, and just at the time I—I found the girl I wanted to marry. It was in my mind, I'll confess. George Gray wanted to kill him, too. We talked it over; we tried to figure out some way in which we could get our money back. That was what George and I were talking about as we walked the streets. I—I lied, because I was frightened. I thought you'd think that I really had killed him."

"And that visit to Mrs. Murphy's?" Haynes suggested. "There were some lies about that, too. Mrs. Murphy tried to tell me that you had asked Miss Dranger to be your wife, and that she had told you to call that evening for your answer, that you called and found the girl out, and did not wait, and that Mrs. Murphy wished you had waited. I ascertained that that was a falsehood, for Miss Dranger told me innocently enough that you never had asked her the important question."

Brown moistened his dry lips, but his gaze did not drop before that of the detective.

"I—I'll tell the truth, sir," he said. "I love Miss Dranger—and I'm not afraid to say it before you all. But I couldn't bring myself to ask her to marry me, because I had lost my money and had only my small business. Lately I had been noticing a man following her, and it worried me. I told Mrs. Murphy about it. Miss Dranger went out at nights alone, nobody knew where. I got the idea that she was in some sort of trouble and I wanted to help her. I confided in Mrs. Murphy. That night Miss Dranger was gone. Mrs. Murphy meant that I should have stayed at her house until we knew for certain that the girl was all right. You see—when a man's in love—— And the man who followed her and watched her was that man sitting over there—the man who calls himself Rathway!"

"Suppose I tell you," said Haynes, "that Mr. Rathway is a member of the government secret service and has been trying to get evidence of fraud on Brayton's part—misuse of the mails? He knew that Miss Dranger's father had been ruined by Brayton in Chicago, and he watched her, I suppose, in the hope that she would lead him to some evidence. He might have thought that Brayton knew her, was afraid of her, and might make some move against her. He may have been watching to protect instead of harm her."

"I—I didn't know," Brown gasped. "Well, I left Mrs. Murphy's at nine thirty, walked around the

streets for a time, and went home and to bed
about eleven. That's the truth. I didn't meet anybody at that time. I haven't an alibi. But I didn't
kill Brayton! You know why I lied, why I refused
to talk much. I didn't want to drag in a girl's
name."

"All right, Brown!" Haynes said brusquely. "We'll
take up George Gray now. Gray had a motive,
and he had an opportunity, because he left Mrs.
Murphy's at nine o'clock. Anything to say, Gray?"

The boy straightened in his chair.

"I never killed him!" he cried. "I was worried
sick because he had robbed me, and Brown and
I were trying to think of some scheme to swindle
him in return and get our money back. When I
left Mrs. Murphy's I went uptown, and walked
up and down Broadway, just worrying and thinking. I came back home about midnight. I—I
can't tell you any more. I haven't an alibi, either.
But I never killed him! I wanted to—at first,
but——"

"That's enough!" Haynes declared. "Madame
Moonshine is next. She could have played The
Scarlet Scourge after leaving Madame Violette's
apartment. And Madame Violette could have played
the part after Madame Moonshine left. Frand, the
janitor, whom Brayton robbed, could have done it.
So could Margaret Dranger, whose father had been
ruined by Brayton, and who was out somewhere
that night until a late hour. One of you, I am
convinced, was The Scarlet Scourge!

"But not all of you would think of a thing like

that or be able to carry such a plan to completion.
Brayton and Satchley were decoyed to their offices
by fake letters mailed in Newark and purporting to
have been sent by a Martin Cogblen, a business
man there. The battery was sent from Newark, too.

"Miss Dranger, you went to Newark one evening
and mailed those letters and that package! Miss
Dranger, you are a stenographer, you have a typewriter in your room, and on the keys of it I found
red ink. You could have written the letter to Brayton, and the red cards used by The Scarlet Scourge.
The question is—were you The Scarlet Scourge
or did you aid the person who was? Did you help
George Brown, who wants to marry you? Did
you help your employer's son? What have you to
say, Miss Dranger? We know your motive—
and you had an opportunity!"

Brown sprang from his chair, his face livid, but
one of the officers forced him back into it again.

"I am waiting for an answer, Margaret Dranger,"
Haynes said in a stern voice.

All eyes were upon the girl now. She looked
up at him fearlessly, though her face had gone
as gray as ashes.

"I—you must be out of your mind, sir," she said.

"Do not evade my question. You mailed those
things in Newark, didn't you? You went over
after dinner, and came back as quickly as possible.
That was the evening Brown returned your purse,
which he had found. Mrs. Murphy lied to him—
said you were tired and had gone to bed. Brown
saw you on the street afterward, and saw Rathway

following you. You see, Brown, Rathway saw you at the same time. How about it, Miss Dranger?"

"I—you must be insane! You never could prove such a thing. Mr. Rathway must have been following some other girl—and I am sure that Mr. Brown was mistaken."

"I am afraid such an answer will do you little good," Haynes said. "How about it, Mrs. Murphy? Why did you tell Brown that Miss Dranger was in bed, when you knew that she was not?"

"Because I didn't want to spoil a love story," Mary Murphy replied instantly. "I knew Brown was falling in love with Margaret, and I knew that she had gone out—and it was ten o'clock and she had not returned. I was afraid Brown would be jealous if I told him that, and it just came into my mind to say that the girl was in bed. I didn't want their romance spoiled—I could see that they were made for each other."

"The stories you people tell get thinner and thinner," Detective Sam Haynes declared. "The person who played The Scarlet Scourge is in this room, and we're going to find out which one of you it is before we leave here."

A sharp knock at the corridor door interrupted him. Detective Haynes crossed the room swiftly, unlocked the door and opened it. The officer on guard in the hall was there, and with him a messenger boy.

"Telegram," he announced.

Haynes looked at the yellow envelope, signed

the boy's book, and closed and locked the door again.

"Message for Margaret Dranger," he said, handing it to the girl. "Read it quickly, please, and then we'll continue our discussion."

Margaret tore open the envelope with trembling fingers. Her face had gone gray again. They saw her read the message swiftly, and then tears came and she began sobbing.

Haynes started toward her. Madame Violette turned toward her, and Mrs. Mary Murphy, the comforting mother personified, started to speak to her.

But Margaret Dranger sprang to her feet, weeping unashamed, agony in her voice when she spoke.

"My father—my father is dead!" she cried. "He died in the sanitarium—because of Lorenzo Brayton. I'll tell now; I don't care! It's all ended! I was The Scarlet Scourge! Do you hear me? I was The Scarlet Scourge!"

CHAPTER XXX

CONFESSION

SHE stood before them all, her hands clenched at her sides, her arms rigid, her chin held high and the tears streaming down her cheeks Mrs. Murphy moved toward her.

"My poor, dear girl!" she said.

"Let me tell it—tell it all now," Margaret implored. "I want to tell it. I've wanted to—because others were accused. But I was afraid before. It doesn't make any difference now—my father is dead."

"Sit down," said Haynes quietly. "Tell us—but try to calm yourself as much as possible. You sit down beside her, Mrs. Murphy, please."

Margaret sat down, and she told her story with Mary Murphy's protecting arm around her shoulders.

"I couldn't endure to have my father in the sanitarium where he couldn't have everything he wanted," the girl said. "The swindlers had left us no money, you see, except a little that I spent trying to find doctors to cure my father. I was working in Chicago, but only making enough to pay for my own living. I began to think that the swindlers should pay!

"I found out all I could about them. I learned that Tampley, as we knew him, had come to New

York and had taken the name of Brayton. Mr. Satchley did not change his name, and I did not learn until later that he had been Brayton's partner in the swindle. But I found it out. I learned that Mr. Satchley always had ten thousand dollars in his safe, enough to help him if he had to run away from the law. I knew that because I heard him talking to Mr. Brayton about it one evening at a restaurant. I was at the next table. I had been watching them for some time, learning all I could about them. You see, I was in New York several weeks before I went to Mrs. Murphy's place.

"Finally I did go to Mrs. Murphy's, and I schemed to get a job in this building, where I could be near Brayton and Satchley. I don't know how the idea of The Scarlet Scourge came into my mind. But I thought about making the cards, so I'd not have to talk and so they couldn't say afterward whether it was a man or a woman.

"Oh, I took plenty of time and figured it all out! I've got a friend who is a stenographer for Mr. Cogblen in Newark. I had gone over to see her a few times, and once when I was in Mr. Cogblen's office I took some of his letterheads out of the desk drawer, and a couple of envelopes.

"I wrote those letters on my machine, and wrote The Scarlet Scourge's letter and the cards, too. And that evening I went over to Newark and mailed the two letters and the battery. I don't know where I got the idea of the battery. But I knew there was no closet in Mr. Brayton's office, and

I knew that he had to be held some way in his office until I could make my escape.

"I felt sure that I would succeed. It was not difficult learning about the two men. You see, when my father was swindled I was away at school, and neither Brayton nor Satchley had seen me. But I was afraid that night. I had the scarlet robe hidden in Madame Violette's place and I slipped into the building and got it, and went through the girls' rest room to the rear stairway, and up the stairs to the floor where Mr. Brayton had his office— this floor.

"There were lights in the office, and I knew that he was there, waiting for the man the letter had said would visit him. I made sure there was nobody else on the floor, then slipped into the gown and entered the office.

"I was frightened when I faced him, but he was not difficult to handle. He was frightened, too, I suppose; probably thought it was somebody he had swindled. I forced him to write the check, made him take hold of the handles of the battery, and then hurried out.

"I went straight up the flight of steps to Mr. Satchley's office, and forced him to cash the check. I escaped easily before Mr. Satchley could get out of the closet. I only wanted the money they had stolen from my father—a part of it—to keep him in comfort so long as he lived. I supposed that Mr. Brayton and Satchley would divide the loss. I thought that it was only fair. But it was useless —for my father is dead now.

"I went down the stairs after I left Satchley's office, and dropped the robe where Frand found it. I had to get on the roof of the little building to the west, and went down a fire escape to the alley, and hurried home. So now you know! I stole the money—and I don't care what you do with me for it! My father is dead and——"

"And Brayton?" Haynes demanded.

"I—I never killed him!" she declared. "I was The Scarlet Scourge, but I never killed him. The weapon I had wasn't even loaded. It's in my room now—it has never been fired—it's a new one. When I saw Mr. Brayton last he was standing before his desk, the handles of the battery in his hands. All I did was to get the ten thousand——"

"Might as well make a clean story of it," Rathway put in. "Sorry you started to confess, are you? The Scarlet Scourge killed Brayton, all right, and you say you are The Scarlet Scourge!"

"I didn't! I couldn't have done it!" Margaret cried. "I stole, but I didn't kill. And the money —it is here!"

She took it from the bosom of her dress, the package of bills still as they were when she had carried them from Satchley's office, and handed the money to Haynes, who tossed it on the table. Haynes had not taken his eyes from the girl's face.

"I—didn't kill him!" she said again.

"Of course she didn't!" Brown cried. "Stop torturing her, will you? Trying to send an innocent girl to prison for life, are you? Trying to make her admit something she never did? She didn't kill him!"

"Did you?" Haynes snapped.

"No! No!" Brown cried. "I don't know who did. But I know Margaret never—she couldn't do such a thing! I knew she was worrying, was in some sort of trouble, and wanted to help her. I want to help her now. I'll always want to help her."

"Brayton was killed, and somebody killed him—somebody in this room!" Haynes insisted. "This girl says that she is The Scarlet Scourge! She held him up in that room in there—had a weapon in her hand——"

"I didn't kill him!" Margaret declared again, sobbing against Mrs. Murphy's bosom.

"We'll let a jury decide that," Haynes said. "There is evidence enough. If you didn't kill him, somebody right in this room did, and that 'somebody' is letting an innocent girl be blamed, letting her face the disgrace of arrest and trial for her life——"

A cry from the other side of the room stopped him. Old Frand hobbled away from the wall, holding out his hands.

"I—I did it!" he cried. "I shot Brayton! I can't see a little girl like that suffer for somethin' I've done!"

CHAPTER XXXI

FRAND TALKS

THEY whirled to look at him, some in surprise, some in horror. Detective Sam Haynes was the only one who did not appear to be startled. Margaret Dranger gasped at him. Rathway's eyes bulged at this unexpected confession.

"Talk!" Haynes commanded.

Frand tottered to the end of the table and sank into a chair there. For a moment he held his head in his hands, and then he raised it and looked Haynes straight in the eyes.

"He—he ruined me," Frand said. "If I'd been a young man, I'd have taken my medicine. But when he first spoke to me about investing my money, I told him it was all I had for my old age, and that if I lost it I didn't know what would become of me. It was only three hundred dollars, you see—but I had saved it a penny at a time, for years and years. I never seemed able to make much money—only got poor wages.

"Can't you understand? It was all I had in the world, and I'm getting old and feeble and can't hold my job much longer. And I haven't a soul to take care of me. I went mad when I learned that he was a swindler. I waited until I was sure that there was no mistake—that the

money was gone. Then I planned to kill him.
It didn't make any difference what they did to
me afterward, for I'm an old man and won't be
able to make a living much longer. If they want—
to take my life—because I took his———"

Frand bowed his head again for a moment, and
the tears rolled down his cheeks. None of the
others in the room spoke a word; they waited for
the old janitor to continue. There was not one,
including Detective Sam Haynes, who did not feel
sorry for Frand.

Presently he raised his head again, and his voice
was more firm, though his hands trembled.

"I got a gun," he went on. "I got an old gun
and oiled it up and bought me some cartridges.
I filled the gun and carried it in one of my pockets,
and waited. Every time I saw Brayton I seemed
to see red. He was well dressed and hired taxi-
cabs—and I was going to starve in my old age.
I determined to kill him. But I thought that I'd
never get a chance. And then—then came that
night!

"I reported at ten o'clock for night elevator work,
you see. We take turns at it in the summer time.
I don't know what made me run the elevator up to
this floor. It—it was just fate, I guess. I thought
that I heard a scream, but maybe I didn't. Anyway,
I came up to this floor, and I saw a light burning
in Brayton's private office. I slipped along the
hall and looked through the keyhole. He was sitting
at his desk, bending over, his back to me.

"I had my janitor's keys, of course. It didn't

take me long to unlock the corridor door of his private office. I got the revolver out of my pocket, too. I opened the door an inch at a time, and watched him closely, but he didn't move. He was looking at some papers, I guess, or maybe he was tired out and asleep.

"It flashed across my mind again what that man had done to me. So I threw up the revolver—and fired. I only fired one shot. Then I shut the door quickly and rushed back to the elevator and went down to the ground floor. It wasn't more than a few seconds after I got there that the bell rang, and I went up to find Mr. Satchley crying that he had been robbed.

"I thought it was all right—that Brayton deserved what I had done to him. I just kept quiet about it, when all the talk of the robbery and of this Scarlet Scourge was going on. I'd have kept quiet forever—only I can't have a little girl blamed for what I did. Here's the gun, sir."

Frand took the ancient revolver from his pocket and handed it to Haynes. The detective looked down at him, and then examined the gun. He extracted one of the cartridges and saw that one had been fired and the weapon not cleaned afterward.

The janitor had broken down now. His head was on his outstretched arms, and he was sobbing. The women were sobbing, too, all except Margaret Dranger. She sat with white face and firm lips, gazing straight ahead of her, as a woman who looks and does not see.

"Think of it!" Brown said, under his breath. "Poor old Frand! That cur of a Brayton——"

Frand's fit of sobbing passed, and he lifted his head again. He looked up at Detective Sam Haynes, and then held out his hands.

"I—I'm ready to go, sir," he said. "I'm ready for you to take me."

Haynes made no move to handcuff the old janitor. He snapped the revolver shut and put it into one of his pockets. Then he glanced down at Frand again, something of pity in his look.

"I—I'm ready to go!" Frand repeated.

"Where?"

"To jail—to prison."

"What for?"

"I killed him! I'm a murderer!"

"Nonsense!" Haynes exclaimed.

A chorus of gasps answered his ejaculation. Every person in the room suddenly had eyes on Haynes instead of Frand.

"What—what do you mean, sir?" Frank gasped.

"You didn't kill Lorenzo Brayton—that's what I mean."

"But I did. I'm not confessing to save anybody else—just because I'm old and worthless. Do you think that, sir? I'm the guilty one. I killed him."

"You think you did," Haynes said, "but you didn't. Lorenzo Brayton was already dead when you fired the shot from this revolver I've got in my pocket. The bullet that killed Brayton is not of the same caliber as this weapon of yours. The bullet you fired didn't strike Brayton at all. You are a bad shot, Frand. The bullet which is identical with those in your revolver went past him and struck the wall just at the edge of one of the filing cases. I found it the last time I examined the office—missed it before that."

"But—but——" Frand began, bewildered, half afraid and half glad.

"You intended to kill him, but you didn't, and so I guess we won't trouble you any about it, Frand."

"You're—you're sure, sir?"

"I'm sure," Detective Sam Haynes said.

"Oh, I'm glad—glad!" old Frand cried. "You don't know how I felt afterward. I didn't want to have a man's blood on my hands—afterward. I'm glad!"

He was weeping again now, but from happiness. Detective Haynes turned from him and surveyed the others.

"What I told Frand is the truth," he said. "I didn't work it out myself until last night. Miss Dranger was The Scarlet Scourge, but she didn't kill Brayton. Frand shot at him, but he didn't kill Brayton."

"Then who did?" Satchley cried.

"The gentleman we know as Mr. Morton Rathway," said Detective Sam Haynes.

CHAPTER XXXII

"THAT'S ALL RIGHT!"

AS he spoke, Detective Sam Haynes whipped his own revolver from its holster and covered the man he had mentioned. Rathway had become very white of face, but now he attempted a laugh.

"Insane, Haynes, or merely playing a game?" he asked.

"Come across the room to me, and keep your hands out of your pockets," Haynes commanded. "Make it snappy!"

Rathway started to advance. "You're a fool!" he blurted out. "This will cost you your job, Haynes. Don't you know——"

"Shut up! I'll do the talking!"

Rathway was close to him now. There was a snap as handcuffs were fastened to Rathway's wrists. He shook them angrily.

"I'll have you kicked off the force for this!" Rathway threatened. "What do you mean by it? Playing some fancy detective game, are you?"

"I'll do the talking," Haynes repeated. "Sit down!"

Rathway sat down beside Frand, who quickly moved away. Rathway was still blustering. He glanced nervously around the room, and saw nothing but expressions of surprise in the faces of the others there. Haynes' face was inscrutable.

"Well?" he asked. "What foolishness are you going to tell us now, Haynes? You police detectives——"

"Keep still!" Haynes exclaimed. "Rathway, while you were waiting in vain for me at Columbus Circle last night, I was searching your room. I had been a little suspicious of you. You were so eager to help me in this case, and so eager to have the crime fastened on Miss Dranger. You appeared to have been watching her a great deal more than an important secret service operative would have done.

"In your rooms I found several things of interest. I found your finger prints on some of your toilet articles, for instance, and the expert at headquarters found the same prints on Brayton's safe and metal filing case. Beneath the carpet in your room I found some papers that had been taken from Brayton's office. I also discovered two small keys, one to the inner compartment of Brayton's safe and the other to the locked filing case. I found a slip of paper with a safe combination written on it—Brayton's safe."

"Of course you found them," Rathway cried. "In my work for the government I got those keys made from impressions I took the day Satchley knocked Brayton unconscious, and I got the combination of the safe from his memorandum book at the same time. I used them to slip in here one night and look for evidence. Those papers you say you found—they are a part of the evidence. You know the job I was on—trying to get the goods on

Brayton for using the mails to defraud.   It was legitimate under the circumstances."

"It was not legitimate," Haynes interrupted him, "for the simple reason that you are not working for the government."

"What's that?"   Rathway was startled.

"I suppose you thought that you were very clever, Rathway.   You made your big talk to the chief and myself about wanting to keep your work a secret even from the other men in your department. You thought, I suppose, that we'd believe you and not make an investigation.   Well, when I became sufficiently suspicious, I used the telephone and called Washington by long distance.   I learned several interesting things about you, Rathway, from the head of the secret service.

"You did work in that line once, and you were working on a case of using the mails to defraud. Among others, Brayton was under suspicion.   But about a year ago you were kicked out of the service, because you attempted to blackmail a man against whom you had evidence.   It was not impossible for you to retain a badge, of course, but those credentials you showed me were forged, Rathway. The chief of the secret service says so."

"This is a mass of lies!"

"It's the truth, and you know it.   Rathway, you were planning to blackmail Brayton.   That's why you asked so many questions about him.   You wanted to find some of his victims and maneuver him into such a position that he would pay you a big sum rather than have you turn him over to the authorities. That is why you got the duplicate keys and the combination of the safe. You went through his filing cases as often as you could. I suppose you entered this office several times at night. It was easy for you, since you had leased an office of your own in the building, and posed as a manufacturer's agent.

"Keep quiet, Rathway—I'm doing the talking now! You were watching Miss Dranger because you thought she was going after Brayton, and possibly you misjudged the girl and had some thoughts of getting an attractive accomplice. Several things she did played right into your hands.

"The night of the crime, you knew nothing of The Scarlet Scourge, of course. After The Scarlet Scourge had gone, Brayton managed to tear his hands away from the battery, which was growing weak. I've had the thing examined, and I know. Brayton rushed into the hall and down the first flight of stairs. He was trying to catch a glimpse of The Scarlet Scourge, of course. Possibly he thought it had been Satchley. His cries had brought no help, and so he started out to summon help.

"He didn't catch sight of The Scarlet Scourge, of course. I suppose his next thought was to rush back to the office and telephone for the police. But while he was gone, you came in, Rathway. The lights in the outer office were extinguished, but one in the private office was burning. It was natural for you to assume that the janitor had neglected to turn it out and to lock the door.

"I suppose the private office looked as though

somebody had been in there recently. But you were inside, and you wanted more of Brayton's papers. You opened the filing case, searched in it, spilled papers on the floor. You opened the safe— and then Brayton rushed back into the office.

"You were discovered Rathway! You're a coward at heart, and fear struck you. You visualized a long prison term—whipped out your revolver—fired almost before you realized what you were doing! Lorenzo Brayton fell, dead! You had shot him through the back as he turned to call for help again, and the bullet had struck through his heart.

"Then you acted foolishly, as most criminals do under stress of emotion. What your idea was, I do not know, but you picked up Brayton's body and seated him in his desk chair, in as natural a posture as possible.

"Almost immediately after, while you were getting out of the building, Frand opened the corridor door and fired at Brayton's body. You escaped from the building while Frand was up here. Frand declared early that he had not been up in the elevator except to take Jones, an attorney, but Frand was lying then to protect himself, of course. That is how it happened, Rathway. Did you think nobody saw you? Did you think that you were fooling everybody around here?"

"Why—why——" Rathway gasped.

"That was it, wasn't it, Rathway?"

"You—you devil!" Rathway cried. "Who saw? How did you know?"

"Not a devil," Haynes corrected. "Just an ordinary police detective assigned to the homicide squad —the newspapers make fun of us sometimes. And really, Rathway—I did not know. I just guessed, worked it out and told the story, and you admitted its truth just now. Nobody saw, either. I suppose your conscience made you admit your guilt. I'd have had a hard time proving it but for your words before all these witnesses."

Haynes stepped to the door and called the policeman stationed there.

"Take this man in, and be careful with him," he directed. "His name is Rathway, and he is charged with the murder of Lorenzo Brayton. The government wants him for impersonating an officer, too, but he's going to the electric chair."

Rathway sprang to his feet, his face livid, struggling like a maniac. But Haynes and the officer subdued him quickly and hurried him into the corridor. Then Haynes came back.

"But I—I stole," Margaret Dranger said, sobbing softly again. "You'd better send me to jail, too."

"I'm sorry," Haynes said. "I suppose the jury will be lenient with you, considering the circumstances."

"And my father—can't I even go to the funeral?"

Haynes had opened the package that The Scarlet Scourge had stolen from Satchley by means of the check Brayton had written. Suddenly he looked up and laughed.

"Counterfeits!" he exclaimed. "Look! Every bill has been stamped as a counterfeit!"

"What?" Satchley cried, springing forward. "It was good money! Brayton—Brayton had that bundle of counterfeits—he used it as a flash roll when he was broke. He knew about that ten thousand in my safe. The crook! He stole the good money long ago, I suppose, and substituted the other. Oh, the crook!"

"I don't think we can do more than hang you for stealing a bundle of counterfeits, young woman, since you have made no effort to pass any of the money," Haynes said. "I think there'll be no charge against you, unless Satchley wants to prefer one because you pointed a gun at him. I'm quite sure that Satchley doesn't want to do that!"

Satchley met his eyes and observed the look on the detective's face.

"I—we'll just let the thing drop," he said.

"Then you are at liberty, Miss Dranger. I'm sorry about your father. You'll want to send a message, I suppose, and to go to Chicago for the funeral. Brown, will you assist her?"

Brown, a little cry of sympathy on his lips, sprang to the girl's side and led her toward the corridor door. The others in the room watched as the couple disappeared, and none failed to notice the look on Brown's face—one that promised lifelong devotion.

"So that's all right," said Detective Sam Haynes softly.

THE END